I0675770

Lost in the Plains

by

H. B. Berlow

*Ark City Confidential Chronicles,
Book Three*

Lost in the Plains

Cover Art by *The Wild Rose Press, Inc.*

The Wild Rose Press, Inc.
PO Box 708
Adams Basin, NY 14410-0708
Visit us at www.thewildrosepress.com

Publishing History
First Mainstream Historical Rose Edition, 2019
Print ISBN 978-1-5092-2796-9
Digital ISBN 978-1-5092-2797-6

Ark City Confidential Chronicles, Book Three
Published in the United States of America

"A German POW walked away from a work detail on a farm in Concordia. The farmer's son was dressed in similar work clothes when the detail returned to the camp."

"We have a POW camp in Concordia?" The chief and I exchanged confused glances.

"We have POW camps all over the United States, Officer Witherspoon. We don't have the resources in terms of manpower to maintain such facilities in the various theaters of war. Most of the prisoners are regulars in the armed forces and not diehard Nazis. Those types are held…elsewhere. For the most part, these soldiers are grateful to be out of harm's way and the local residents have found it beneficial to have additional labor at a very low cost. These men are not a danger to the citizens."

"Except for one of them who just didn't feel like returning to his gilded cage."

"Yes, well, that's why we're here."

"But he's not a danger to the citizens."

"We don't believe so."

With a smile as wide as Joe E. Brown, I replied, "I'm sorry, guys. I think I'm missing something here. A German soldier, who's not a danger to the citizens, walks off a farm in Concordia and you think he's coming all the way down here to Ark City?"

Praise for H. B. Berlow

"In the '30s, all towns and most cities had very little documentation required for police activity. Hell, around here as recently as the '70s you could arrest a felon by filling out a 3x5 index card with a simple narrative on the back. And it was perfectly legal to shoot and kill a felon if they didn't stop when you told them to. (That didn't change in the South until 1984.) So you are spot on with having your character concentrate on the street instead of worrying about lawsuits and heat from the brass."

~James Montgomery, Officer,
Garland County, Arkansas
Sheriff's Department (retired),
on Ark City Confidential

~*~

"H.B. Berlow writes with an extraordinary imagination expressed in a provocative crime thriller containing unforgettable characters."

~Dr. Bruce Lindsay, Police commissioner,
Rochester, New Hampshire (retired),
on Secrets of the Righteous,
Ark City Confidential Chronicles, Book Two

Dedication

To Charlotte Gloria (Entin) Berlow and Beth Alhadeff:
two gracious ladies from World War II

Acknowledgments

My gracious thanks to Paul Rimovsky of the Camp Concordia WWII German POW Camp Museum for his knowledge and guidance.

Chapter One

It had been windy with a light frost, hardly any snow for early December. Nothing like years past with swirling winds and foot-high snow banks. Just chilly enough for gloves and ear muffs. Dave Morton had gone to the Burford to watch the matinee of *Sergeant York* with Gary Cooper when they stopped the show just five minutes into it. The manager came on stage and announced the Japanese had bombed Pearl Harbor. Dave raced back to the station and blabbered incoherently to turn on the radios. Several of us just sat there with our mouths open and wondered how this could ever happen. The next day, Roosevelt delivered the official message, declared it a "day of infamy" and told us we were already at war. I was ready to go.

An Irish entertainer and an Irish gangster both convinced me to fight the Hun in the Great War. George M. Cohan said it was for the benefit of my country; Dion O'Banion claimed it was good for my character. I got my face entangled in barbed wire and earned scars that became a mask for a new identity. There were too many times where my old life reached like a ghost into the present day.

For over twenty years, I had been Baron Witherspoon, farm boy turned soldier turned beat cop in Arkansas City, Kansas. Eric Kimble from the North Side Gang, the guy I used to be, was a distant but persistent memory. Therefore, it became an instinct to serve my country. Of course, the draft board, headed up by Dr. Louis Brenz, declared me 4F. My age (43) and my importance as an officer of the law were the reasons given. They didn't have to mention my face looked like it started to melt off my skull on account of the surgery that, at the time, was new and progressive but now seemed like something from the Dark Ages. Dr. Brenz told me many times only some new surgery, whenever it was developed, could prevent the skin from sagging any further. As long as I didn't mind looking fifteen years older, I just wasn't going to count on going under the knife again.

Since I couldn't go back and fight the Hun again, I continued to walk my beat in hopes of keeping my small Kansas city safe. Then I became an air raid warden and offered to help with rubber drives and paper drives and scrap metal drives and just about any drive to collect anything for the war effort. I collected kitchen fat and old rags. Heck, I even encouraged a banker and a couple of politicians to buy war bonds. I didn't realize I was that good of a salesman. The irony was I wanted to go to war because I felt it was necessary for the country and not just for me. Everything I had been through led me to this time. Not a gangster from the old neighborhood or a sweet sad girl on a mission for vengeance could deter me from my path. I had become a patriot and a man of honor. Funny how twenty years changed someone.

All these years later, Jake Hickey even impacted Dave Morton's life. The bullet in the shoulder he took from that crazy gangster back in '34 forced him to sit out the war as well. Seems he could no longer raise his arm over his head. Something to do with damage to the muscles. The jokes about not being able to play tennis anymore became stale after the umpteenth time. He and I continued on with our daily lives but with a greater sense of urgency, as it was with everyone else. The refineries worked round the clock as well as the mills. Any pilot, from a crop duster to a barnstorming fool, got involved in the war effort, some as trainers for young guys who didn't know thrust from lift or drag. There was rationing of gasoline and belt tightening from all the residents I had a chance to talk with. The farmers had to produce even more crops, raising more livestock, to feed the nation and supply the troops. Farming was already a difficult life. I remember when I came back from the war, and Baron's real father took me in because he believed I was his son and hoped I would follow in his footsteps. Didn't take to it then. Now, a lot of the smaller farmers found it hard to keep up.

I ran into Joe Pajak early in the spring of '42. He had a small spread on the south end of town, mostly soybeans and wheat. One day I helped him load his truck with supplies.

"You hear old Mongo McAllister made himself a Doodlebug?" he asked.

"A what?" It was not a common expression from the North Side of Chicago, that much was certain.

"He took a '22 Model A Ford and turned it into a tractor. Now he's got two. I gotta get him to help me build one or I ain't never gonna bring in a good crop."

Because of the war effort and the shortages of supplies, everyone did what they had to. There was no other choice. Sandy Clevenger, the long-time secretary at the *Ark City Traveler* conducted weekly paper drives and sold bonds as though she had been doing it all her life. Not knowing anything about her before her time at the newspaper, it was possible she had been a grifter.

Mrs. Banister sold the house where I lodged for so many years to the U.S. Department of the Army to quarter soldiers who came into the area. She wound up moving back to Wichita to be with her daughter. I was sad to see her go. I knew I was going to miss her lemon bars and chocolate zucchini bread as well as the closest thing I had to a mother. There were plenty of sacrifices to go around.

Because of it, I was out of a home. The Gladstone Hotel became a sanitarium and then reverted to the Highland Hotel before it was renamed the Elmo Hotel. I wound up living there. It was less than ten years ago Jake Hickey and his lady, Heather Devore, holed up two floors above me, waiting for the heat to cool off in Chicago when Capone and Moran were going at it, before he realized he had been dumped like yesterday's trash. The irony was rather thick. A deadly gangster from my youth swaggered around these halls. I had similar accommodations to those in Mrs. Banister's house. Primarily a bed, a dresser, a writing table and chair, and a closet. There weren't too many things I owned, and I preferred it that way. There was nothing much to interest me, no hobbies and no one special in my life. I just tended to sit in my room and read the newspaper or listen to the radio when I wasn't walking a beat.

A year and several months later, the military of the United States was participating all over the globe. Lee Jones signed up after his buddy and former Ark City cop Jay Davis enlisted. While stationed over in England, they wrote letters complaining about the food. It was just like those boys. They had all the enthusiasm in the world. I just hoped they would use their heads to keep themselves out of trouble.

By this time, Daisy Mae's was always crowded with new refinery and mill workers arriving as well as pilots training at the Strother Field Auxiliary #5 just west of town. The kid she hired several years ago, Ralph Houseman, really earned his stay with both cleaning and maintenance. Dixie even brought back old Ashley Watts, who had retired after slinging hash for thirty-five years. With a pencil behind her ear and bright red lipstick that served as a beacon, this grandmother served it up as fast as it came through the kitchen window.

Chief Richardson insisted while the war brought folks together in all these efforts, it didn't mean crime would just disappear. In spite of his constant briefings, it seemed like there were bank robberies south of us in Tulsa and up in Wichita and nothing much going on in our neck of the woods.

The rest of the world was on fire, but it was rather quiet in Ark City.

Chapter Two

I got a postcard from Jeannette Ross, who was still in San Francisco. She was a headliner and really drawing in the crowds in some theater I had never heard of. Then again, I wasn't too familiar with the one she was performing at in Wichita when I asked her to be a target for a killer. Recently, she did some work with the USO. Navy boys, either training or in the hospital, were pleased to have her come by and sing a song or dole out donuts and coffee, maybe a peck on the cheek and a photo as a keepsake. However, I'm sure the military brass weren't too keen on her fan dancing. After all, this was supposed to be a wholesome war.

The *Wichita Daily Beacon* had more national and international news than the *Ark City Traveler*. Sandy Clevenger tended to give me a funny look when she'd catch me reading another rag. I came across an article about Shep Breckman doing shows over in North Africa. He got strafed by enemy aircraft while performing, the peace of an afternoon rudely interrupted by unexpected Axis visitors. Back in Wichita in '38, he seemed oblivious to everything around him except his own future success. This was just the kind of public relations event to catapult Shep into the limelight once the war ended. I guess it was a small price to pay for the glamour and fame of Hollywood.

Out of nowhere, two guys wearing suits only

Federal agents would wear walked in like they owned the city, went directly to the chief's office, knocked and walked in, and sat with their backs to the glass window. To my way of thinking it would seem like they would want some privacy, given that's how I had a notion the way G-men worked. But when I walked by a couple of times, I caught the chief's eye and realized he might be looking for a parachute to break his fall. I wasn't going to let him down.

Acting like the rube they expected all of us to be, I simply barged in as though I didn't have a care in the world and blind to boot.

"Chief, about those reports..." I gave them my best Jimmy Stewart look, all shy and embarrassed, with a little "shucks, golly" and kicking the floor with my foot thrown in for good measure.

"Oh. Come on in, Witherspoon," the chief beckoned. I came alongside, and he directed his comments to the two men looking somewhat perturbed at the intrusion. "Gentlemen, this is Officer Baron Witherspoon. Been on the department since..."

"1920, sir." I stood at attention, pride oozing out of my schoolboy smile, like Mickey Rooney wanting to be a junior G-man or put on a backyard musical.

"Officer Witherspoon was instrumental in the capture of gangster Jake Hickey back in '34..."

"As well as consulting with both Eliot Ness in the Kingsbury Run murders and the Wichita Police Department on their Ripper slayings in 1938." The heavyset agent looked like he could tear limbs from bodies, but his face was whiter and softer than a newborn's back end. He spoke with the voice of a college professor or a librarian, but he sounded bored at having to let us know what he knew to prevent an extended conversation. This meeting was apparently not about me.

"So, you know all about me." I wasn't taunting so much as wondering what they actually knew.

"We know everything." He turned his attention back to Chief Richardson as though I had just become invisible. "As we discussed, Chief Richardson…"

"This is Special Agent Hollis Burke," the chief said, interrupting again and pointing to the man who had dismissed me, "and Special Agent Alexander Gordon." Maybe the chief was trying to buy time to think of how to handle the situation. I never knew him to be like that, but the way these guys just barged in would have put anyone off their game. If there was supposed to be some professional courtesy it didn't appear to exist in the room.

Gordon appeared to be older than mid-thirties but only because of the anger hidden behind clear blue eyes. Then again, I might have mistaken more boredom for anger. His blondish hair was tinged with bits of brown and his face looked windblown. Perhaps it was just him getting used to Kansas. Neither one extended a welcoming hand.

"We're not interested in making our presence here widely known, Chief." Burke continued like a slow-moving train. It was apparent he wasn't used to small town police departments and felt he could use the weight and authority of the federal government to get unabated cooperation. He didn't know Lester Richardson.

"Gonna be kinda hard with those suits." I knew vaudeville was dead, but I couldn't resist. Nevertheless, we needed to make a point, and I knew the chief would rather have me make it than undermine his position on the force. "Let's be honest, guys. You come into a small Kansas town dressed like gangsters from the North Side of Chicago and expect to blend in and go unnoticed? Seems to me like most folks would think you were the bad guys. All we've got to go on is the picture show."

Burke and Gordon had what amounted to a non-verbal discussion, looking at each other as though it were a secret code. Burke proceeded with his college lecture.

"A German POW walked away from a work detail on a farm in Concordia. The farmer's son was dressed in similar work clothes when the detail returned to the camp."

"We have a POW camp in Concordia?" The chief and I exchanged confused glances.

"We have POW camps all over the United States, Officer Witherspoon. We don't have the resources in terms of manpower to maintain such facilities in the various theaters of war. Most of the prisoners are regulars in the armed forces and not diehard Nazis. Those types are held...elsewhere. For the most part, these soldiers are grateful to be out of harm's way and the local residents have found it beneficial to have additional labor at a very low cost. These men are not a danger to the citizens."

"Except for one of them who just didn't feel like returning to his gilded cage."

"Yes, well, that's why we're here."

"But he's not a danger to the citizens."

"We don't believe so."

With a smile as wide as Joe E. Brown, I replied, "I'm sorry, guys. I think I'm missing something here. A German soldier, who's not a danger to the citizens, walks off a farm in Concordia and you think he's coming all the way down here to Ark City?"

Burke pulled out his notebook, more for effect than anything else because I gathered he knew this case intimately. His efforts to impress me were no more effective than Ward Bond trying to impress Humphrey Bogart in "The Maltese Falcon."

"The soldier, Eihan Hammerschmidt, was working on the farm of one John Schneiter."

"German guy?" I interrupted, much to his dismay.

"Schneiter is a first generation U.S. citizen. However, the family is from Weimar. Hammerschmidt was an ordnance officer, trained in explosives. He has a sister who left Germany as a child and lives in Tulsa."

"And all that adds up to Ark City?" I prided myself in my ability to reason through a situation. I had researched violent crimes in both Ark City and Wichita and through deduction was able to determine a killer in each case. These federal agents had their own logic that went completely over my head. Maybe I was wet behind the ears when it came to a complex case like this, but the least I could do was try to understand it, if only for the good of the people of Arkansas City.

"You have the recently completed Strother Field and you have refineries."

"Tulsa's got airfields. Tulsa's got refineries." I shrugged my shoulders for emphasis, even though I was no Ward Bond or Joe E. Brown.

"Hammerschmidt is too smart to go somewhere that would be a trap. No, Officer Witherspoon, our sights are set here. We have reliable intelligence that would make this town a target for an act of sabotage."

"You have reliable intelligence," I repeated. It almost felt like vaudeville was making a comeback.

I glanced at Chief Richardson briefly. It was difficult to determine if his look of concern was true or feigned. Neither of us had much experience with the Feds, even me with my limited involvement in the North Side Gang, so we didn't know what to make of all their bluster. By the same token, we weren't going to just let these guys walk all over us.

"Well, and how do you plan to proceed?" The chief took back some of his authority the agents sucked out of the room by their imposing authority. He sounded once again like the tactician he had become.

"Hammerschmidt is not going to be able to commit any acts of sabotage without the support of others. He more than likely has a contact within your town." I resisted the urge to argue with him, since it was obvious they considered themselves to be right. Probably all the time. And besides, what did our small police department know about sabotage? "We're going to take up at the Elmo Hotel and conduct our own investigation. On the Q.T." The smile was more like a smirk, as though he realized they were going to be a splinter in our side and relished the idea.

"How can we be of assistance?" I hate to admit it, but there was a touch of hopefulness in my voice. However, I was too old to be that naïve.

"Our visit with Chief Richardson was largely a courtesy, Officer Witherspoon. You can help us best by staying out of our way."

Burke nodded, stood, and left. Then Gordon

followed him without uttering a word. Chief Richardson and I exchanged glances, then watched the two special agents leave. We were to be nothing more than an audience to what could turn out to be a comedy or a tragedy.

****

Camp Concordia—Arrival

Members of the 456th Military Police Escort Guard Company as well as the 457th MPEG arrived at Camp Concordia on July 3, 1943. The first four hundred prisoners arrived on July 15. Even with 169 civilian employees, the prisoners slightly outnumbered their captors. No one in the military or the government had given that statistic much consideration. It was initially determined this would be a largely non-confrontational interment camp.

The majority of the prisoners were from Rommel's Deutsche Afrika Corps. Several members of the 15th Panzer Division were among the first group. After suffering heavy casualties at the Battle of Kasserine Pass in February, they surrendered along with other Axis forces in Tunisia in May. The Tunisian Campaign turned out to be a long, brutal six months for both sides.

This new camp was situated north of the Kansas town of Concordia. Faces of anticipation and uncertainty lined the railroad track as the POWs passed through. Residents were not exactly sure what to expect, in spite of the political posturing. There was no further interrogation or interview among the men, no inquiry as to political alliance or Nazi affinity. Many of the men, despite the comfort of this journey, were in poor physical condition, whether underweight or suffering from malnutrition. The first intention of the captors was to ensure the prisoners' well-being. This was per the guidelines of the Geneva Convention, which were to be adhered to in the strictest manner.

Oberfeldwebel Eihann Hammerschmidt accompanied Pvt. Paul Boehmler and Pvt. Erich Loeher through the initial interrogations in Oran, through the passage on the Liberty ships, and on the coach trains from Camp Shanks, New York. The younger enlisted men were barely in their twenties, had no stomach for war, and were rather pleased they were captured. Hammerschmidt was first and foremost a soldier and always kept his eyes in the correct direction.

"They're not finished," he said aloud, to no one in particular, then suddenly became annoyed with himself for even speaking. He was in his late twenties, with bright blond hair and a face that appeared chiseled from a quarry, one that had evolved through struggles and determination. He rarely smiled but never looked mean or domineering because of it. The world at large was too serious a place for frivolity.

"What do you mean?" Loeher inquired.

"This does not look like a fully functional camp. There are not sufficient guards for adequate confinement. Some of those outer buildings are still under construction. Perhaps they do not care if we escape."

"But where would we go?" Boehmler questioned.

These young men had only to wait in relative comfort, given the inconveniences and lack of amenities in North Africa, for what would surely be a victory for the Allied forces, and then sent home. Hammerschmidt had other plans. They did not include interment in a roughshod POW camp. There was still a mission to follow.

Major Armin Steinbauer gathered the men of the 15th and 10th Panzer Divisions, as they currently had no CO. He would wind up housed in the officers' barracks in a bit more comfort than the enlisted men. Still, these facilities did not appear anywhere as harsh as he knew their counterparts were experiencing in Germany. For that he was entirely grateful.

"I have it on good faith, men, the U.S. troops plan to extend us every courtesy per the Geneva Convention. We have fought a good fight, but we have lost to greater forces. I recommend you find a way to co-exist with our captors, perhaps take the opportunity to work on their farms. I know many of you have come from homes where tilling the soil was your livelihood. Make of this place a home until the war ends."

Hammerschmidt was disgusted. The German Army was a place where boys were forged into men, and here was an officer encouraging them to be lambs because it was the easiest thing to do. The war was not over, despite the feelings of many regular army soldiers. While North Africa may have been lost, Rommel was still commanding Panzer divisions in Europe. He heard whispers of resistance plots but kept his distance from them. There was no time to consider what was happening elsewhere in the world. He had locked away in his head alternate plans and a secret directive. The incompletely constructed camp and the numbers advantage meant he would have to work quickly before circumstances changed.

This was a strange time for Hammerschmidt. He had another assignment, unbeknownst to his commander. He could tell no one else. He had no names or direct associates for assistance. He had only one or two targets and an approximate notion of who could assist him should it be required. Taken as a whole, it was most assuredly a suicide mission. But then again, it was for *Deutschland über alles*, so the consequences were unimportant as long as he achieved his goal. He was a man of immeasurable skill; an ordnance man who could fashion an explosive device from various and sundry materials and cause a disturbance in the Allied war effort. That was his only mission. This camp in the middle of rural Kansas was but a small intrusion.

Hammerschmidt went to work. He found a bunk and figured out where to put his contraband: an *Offiziersmesser* or army knife; a compass; a small roll of 40 g/m detonating cord; and a Zippo lighter found on the body of a dead American soldier in the early phases of the Battle of Kasserine Pass. These items would certainly not add to his comfort in the camp. They would, however, become useful tools as he attempted to complete his mission.

While each of the items was instrumentally important, he determined to hide them separately so the loss of one would not be as impactful as the loss of all. By themselves, they represented no immediate threat, outside of the detonating cord. He looked closely in the direction of his bunk and footlocker, toward the wall behind it, across the room, everywhere there might be a safe location a guard would not find and, more important, a fellow soldier would not question. A spare pair of shoes in a footlocker, a pillow of his bunkmate, the bottom of a pack of cigarettes which were never empty, and a small hot water bottle were inconspicuous enough. At this point in time, he didn't need them; he just didn't want to lose them.

He walked around as much of the compound as possible and memorized locations of buildings and guard towers. He calculated distances using only his steps. The lines of sight from each tower were a consideration as well as the schedule of the guards themselves. He had tried to focus clearly on the landscape as the train traveled west from New York, but too many distractions by the seemingly happy German soldiers made it difficult for him to pay attention. He knew largely the town was closer to the northern edge of the state, perhaps closer to Nebraska than to Oklahoma, which is where he needed to be. He had no indication of distance and assumed for the moment he would have to hike a fair distance to get to his destination.

When the guards came with the prison garb, he realized his challenges had increased. The letter P stitched on each arm of the shirt and each leg of the pants stood out as boldly as the A on the skirt of Hester Prynne. Once he was able to determine how he would leave the camp, there was now the burden of new clothing to avoid detection. No matter the distance, he would stand out as a stranger in a strange land.

Eihann had to walk a distance to the latrine. A guard followed him visually. Eihann smiled. The guard didn't smile back. So much for the Geneva Convention.

He looked across the compound and saw three very young and very attractive ladies, girls really, going into what appeared to be an administration building. He began to understand the reactions of such soldiers as Boehmler and Loeher. This place certainly was no paradise, but compared to the brutality of war, it contained many pleasant diversions.

Those were something he did not need.

He continued smiling and nodding at the guards he passed, careful not to let anyone know his mastery of English. This might have made them think he was a spy, so it was necessary for him to speak German only and play dumb. To his way of thinking, this was, after all, what most of the Americans thought of them. What he was able to gather was fit men would be allowed to work on farms as Major Steinbauer had indicated. It was to be perhaps the only opportunity he had before guard levels were increased and the U.S. military erected more walls and wire. Time was always going to be a factor.

As much as it sickened him to kowtow to the effete officer, he had to make it known to Steinbauer he was willing to cooperate, at least as far as they were concerned. The quicker he got an assignment to a work detail, the sooner he would be able to gather more information to plan an escape.

"I would have thought you might have resisted such an offer, Hammerschmidt," the major said smugly. "Once a solder, always a soldier, huh?"

"It would not be possible for me to simply while away the hours interminably. Who knows how long we might be here? Besides, *ein gesunder Körper ist ein gesunder Geist*, a healthy body is a healthy mind. Isn't that what officers usually preach, Major?"

It was a performance that would have made Hans Albers proud.

"Good attitude. I will advise the sergeant in charge of assigning work details to include you in the first group."

Hammerschmidt nodded affirmatively and started to walk off. He hid a smile of satisfaction.

"Oberfeldwebel," Steinbauer called.

"Yes, Major."

"Do you not have, I believe, a sister in these parts?"

"Yes, Major. In Tulsa. In the state of Oklahoma."

"How far is it from here?"

"I could not hazard a guess, Major."

"Shouldn't you get a letter to her, let her know your whereabouts?"

"In due time, sir. Thank you for your consideration." This level of polite courtesy began to nauseate him.

It occurred to him his sister could be useful in this endeavor. Were he able to escape the camp and elude detection, his sister's location would be considered his ultimate destination and throw the authorities off track. Prior letters sent to her were designed to give the impression of his longing for a reunion. It would become necessary to mention her frequently to anyone who would listen. He needed to hide his ultimate target as well as he could. The sister who left Germany because she could not stomach being German was to be, in some obtuse fashion, an unwitting ally. War is known for creating strange ironies.

However, in order to communicate, he would have to allow for his capacity to speak English to come out. Again, he would use whatever drama skills at his disposal to play the caricature of the simple submissive German soldier.

It was the next morning he encountered a guard, a

metal badge referencing Pvt. Stangel, and was quick to offer a light from a box of matches. It was the first time he had seen any guard smile. Stangel nodded graciously.

"You speak English?" the guard inquired. Hammerschmidt held his thumb and forefinger apart yet close.

"I like be in America. No more war." Stangel nodded in understanding, figuring most of these guys were happy to be out of harm's way. "I have sister."

"You have a sister?"

"*Ja.* Yes. She's here."

"Here?" Stangel asked pointing down, as though she were at their feet. The conversation was passing like a man talking to a dog and assuming he understood. The German soldier nodded his head negatively.

"Where is, um, Tulsa?" Hammerschmidt projected the naïveté of a dolt. He said the name of the city as though he were uncertain it even existed.

"Oh, that's in Oklahoma," Stangel responded, as though all Germans had a grasp of U.S. geography.

"How far?"

"I'd say about three hundred miles." Hammerschmidt looked confused. Stangel finally figured it was a different method of distance than what the Germans used. "Probably less than five hundred kilometers." The German nodded in understanding.

"I see her maybe?"

"Oh, I don't know about that. But you will be able to write her a letter."

"That's good." He kept nodding and repeating the words as he backed away. A man with an IQ in excess of 150 with an engineering degree from the University of Stuttgart behaved like a slave in the American Civil War. Just another of the many sacrifices to be made in the name of the war effort.

Chapter Three

I sat in Burke's seat and stretched my feet out, clasping my hands at the back of my neck. Unless I was mistaken, agents from the Federal Bureau of Investigation were intentionally excluding a local police department in its entirety from a search for a possible saboteur, an individual who could potentially cause great harm to the citizens of our city. On top of that, there was an unfounded accusation a resident was a conspirator. I wasn't sure whether to yell or spit.

"How do you want to handle this, Chief?" I asked, taking the high road. I guess being older had somewhat softened my disposition.

Chief Richardson stared straight ahead at nothing, or at least not at anything I could see. His eyes were squinted and focused, fingertips touching delicately yet looking like he was ready to ball his fists. This didn't set well with him either. From a night patrolman in '26 to becoming Chief in '34, he had worked hard to keep the town clean. While I had been on the force longer, he and I differed in that he was destined to move up the ranks and I was simply hiding. He respected the residents and couldn't accept such a proposition as low and uninformed as what he had just heard.

"Put together a team of three other men. Morton, obviously. He's practically been your right hand since those gruesome murders. I'd reach out to Marcus Hayes as well."

"That old relic?" Hayes was pushing sixty-five, with a face like a saddlebag yet still not as bad as mine. A gruff, tobacco-chewing, no-nonsense guy who survived three shootings, two while with other police departments, he could have been higher up the chain if his attitude would have allowed it.

"He's tough as nails and loves this city. Take Evan Cobb, too." Cobb was college educated and married with two kids. He moved to Ark City from Salina on account of his wife getting a job as a teacher down here. I didn't know him as much, as he'd only been on the force two months. The chief's recommendation was good enough for me. "Conduct your own investigation. See what you come up with. You still got connections with Ness?"

After his stint as the Public Safety Director in Cleveland, where he failed to bring in the Kingsbury Run killer, Ness got divorced, was involved in a high-profile car accident, and finally remarried before moving to Washington. I had sent him a telegram to congratulate him on his new marriage, but that was four years ago. As far as I knew, he still thought well of me.

"Another thing," Chief Richardson continued. "Try to find this sister in Tulsa. She's either an innocent pawn or part of this game."

"And if she is a part of it?"

"Your job, Officer Witherspoon, is to protect and serve the people of Arkansas City, Kansas. I'll let the Hoover boys take care of the rest of the country."

I quietly located Morton, Hayes, and Cobb and "invited them to lunch" at Daisy Mae's. If we met in a conference room at the station, it would have looked suspicious, causing tongues to wag, which might have gotten back to the G-men. Ralph Houseman brought water glasses and took our orders.

"You waiting tables now?" I asked.

"Tabatha is out sick, and Rachel's tending to her baby. So—" There was nothing more to say. A good-natured kid, he didn't seem to mind filling in. Sort of became someone you could count on for any occasion.

Dixie came over right before the plates were brought out.

"You boys figuring out a way to knock out that goose stepper?" She knew perfectly well two guys with ailments, an old guy, and a married man were left out of the party. It didn't mean we couldn't fight the war right here in Kansas.

"Nah. Just figuring a way to keep you safe, Dixie."

She laughed hard from the belly.

"You just worry about yourselves." She walked off just as the fattest burgers this side of Kansas City were plopped down on the table.

"Whatever we do," I stated in between bites, "can't be shared with anyone but Chief Richardson."

"I don't understand." Evan Cobb was perhaps the best thinker among the four of us. I sure could have used him in '35 with the killings in Ark City and in '38 when Wichita had their Ripper murders.

"The federal boys don't want our help trying to locate a possible saboteur in our own city. I don't know why, and I don't much care. So we're going to do whatever it takes to keep Ark City safe without them." The level of maturity and responsibility I heard in my own voice was nothing like the tough Eric Kimble from the North Side of Chicago or the quiet and peaceful farm boy that had been Baron Witherspoon. After all these years I had become my own person, cobbled from two separate and distinct men. I still wasn't totally sure who that new man might be.

"Do we just sit and wait?" I could always count on Dave Morton to be eager for anything risky, even after getting shot by a gangster.

"No, we don't. Marcus, I want you to head up to Concordia. Meet with the prison officials, the county sheriff, even that farmer, John Schneiter. I think they'll be able to relate to a good old country boy."

"Who are you talking about?" he barked.

"You."

"Son, what you know about me could fill a thimble. I was born in K.C., on the Missouri side. City boy all the way. All I know of cows is they give milk, which I used to drink as a kid."

I had to smile. "Trust me. They'll relate to you all the same. Evan, I want you to do an analysis of possible targets in the area. Not just Ark City but Tulsa, Oklahoma City, Joplin, Springfield, and Wichita."

"That's a tall order."

"Yeah, I know. But we've got to start somewhere. And I've got an equally tall order for you, Dave."

"What's that?"

"Find Hammerschmidt's sister in Tulsa. We've got to figure out if she's part of this or just a decoy of some sort. Might have to reach out to the War Department. Get Linda Kuchenberg to call from the station. It makes it sound more official."

"And you?" Dave asked.

"I need to locate some old friends who might be helpful."

It was a full nine years since I last encountered Abram Dutcher, known as Der Kaiser, the former head of all criminal activity in Arkansas City before the Great War started. He often used to communicate through Karla Frankl, a perennially mean-looking woman who I always thought could chew through a steel bar. Germans were the enemy now, and the likelihood of them being around, much less out in the open, was slim to none. I still needed to locate him and see what he knew.

There were a few good old boys who brought messages as well as food and supplies out to a squatter's shack far east out of town, just after Parker Cemetery. It was a fitting place for a woman who was part of the living dead. I couldn't imagine Karla Frankl having any reason for living beyond the fact she was just too plain stubborn to die.

Only a full moon lit me as I stood in the doorway. Her eyes grew large, although they still appeared sleepy and fatigued, with dark circles and heavy lines like a mask. In that regard, we weren't too different from each other.

"I hope you brought more than just your charming good looks." Her accent seemed even thicker. Perhaps the weariness of age does that to you. I held forth a bag with dried meat, bread, apples, and a bottle of wine that a bartender at Junior's said was German. She smiled upon seeing the label, took a big bite from the apple, and motioned me forward.

"You risk much by coming here," she said cryptically.

"You risk much by being here."

"The answer to the riddle is Death. The riddle itself

is of no importance." I took a heavy breath and exhaled. She was wiser than she appeared. I was surprised but grateful.

"I need to see him. I need his advice."

She looked at me quizzically, eyebrow raised, nostrils flaring.

"What makes you think he's still alive?"

"Because you are. Because you are only living to continue to serve him. You wouldn't have the gall to die before him." To be perfectly honest, I didn't know if what I was saying was accurate. All I had to go on was an impression from nine years earlier. At this point, I only had my instincts to trust, since the truth was not apparent.

The laugh was hearty and filled with phlegm, raspy and sick, a person who had one foot firmly planted on the other side. Nevertheless, it was an indication she was, indeed, still alive. And so was Dutcher.

"He will find you."

That's all I needed. As I reached the doorway, she called back to me, "What? No wine glass?"

Karla Frankl would never give up the ghost without a fight and a spit in the eye. For that matter, the final word.

****

Camp Concordia—Work Detail

Sergeant Price and Private Friebus of the 457th MPEG oversaw the assignment of the first work detail. Price had dark hair and a perennially serious demeanor. An Abbott and Costello movie would likely give him heartburn. Friebus had sandy blond hair, the likes of which could fit in with the prisoners he guarded. That didn't go unnoticed by the young soldier from Goddard,

26

Kansas. It was Wednesday, July 7. The prisoners had been there less than a week. Due to the unusually small number of available guards, the initial crew was fifteen prisoners that were evenly divided between local residents Charles Blosser, Henry Baxa, and John Schneiter. Baxa's farm was located in Agenda, Kansas, about thirteen miles northwest of the camp. It would take at a minimum thirty-five minutes to get there. As such, three guards were assigned to the five men heading out there. Blosser and Schneiter had property closer to Concordia. It was determined only one guard would be required for each of those units.

****

Major Steinbauer, through the Adjutant, Lieutenant Zander, was able to recommend Hammerschmidt to be one of the original fifteen. He made some reference to Hammerschmidt becoming easily bored, a subtle implication he could turn into a troublemaker if not kept busy. Had Eihann known this, he would have blown a gasket. The major's other motive was to keep Hammerschmidt away as he felt him to have what he considered "subordinate traits." Steinbauer was going to maintain whatever comforts he could even if it meant those of his underlings.

****

The five prisoners assigned to Schneiter's farm were loaded into an open-air truck that regrettably did not have seats. Private Friebus was the lone soldier to oversee this crew. When they arrived, Schneiter leaned in at the back and looked over the five men. All seemed eager and strong.

"*Meine Herren, ich spreche fließendes Deutsch. Wir sind hier für eine Arbeitsbeziehung. Lassen Sie uns diese Zeit konstruktiv verbringen.*" (Gentlemen, I speak fluent German. We are here for a working relationship. Let us spend this time constructively.)

Hammerschmidt was impressed. While he recognized this man might have been simply intelligent, he speculated he had a German background of some kind. As such, he immediately recognized the possibilities inherent in this fortunate work detail placement. A good deal of luck would be beneficial if this secondary mission were to have any degree of success. Now was as good a time for it to start.

The initial work was harvesting crops: mostly wheat but also tomatoes and potatoes as well as a variety of berries many wives made into jams for sale. Eihann assumed the infusion of labor was helpful to the many farmers who saw available workers enlist in the war. The irony was the prisoners were actually aiding in the war effort. While he didn't see it that way, passing the time in this manner was better than sitting and staring at the walls. There would be payment for working as well as educational classes in subjects like English, theology, and architecture for which they could receive certificates. His fellow prisoners each recognized how fortunate they were. He did as well, but for a different reason.

Just before noon, Mrs. Schneiter brought out a platter of ham-and-cheese sandwiches. Her son, Arthur, only fourteen but as tall as most of the prisoners, stopped for a moment to help his mother by carrying a tray with a pitcher of lemonade and glasses. The men sat where they could, on bales of hay or a tractor, ate their sandwiches, and enjoyed the cold beverage. Eihan and the others barely made eye contact with the

Schneiters or even themselves and didn't speak. In spite of the pride in their work, the fresh air, and the food, they were still prisoners and knew they were required to behave or else they might lose this privilege.

Hammerschmidt watched Schneiter as he approached the private as he was finishing his lunch.

"Private Friebus, will these men have something other than prison garb to wear?"

"Yes, sir. We've been a little behind in getting all the necessary supplies and such. But by the first of next week, we should have appropriate work clothing for them."

Eihann overheard this. To be able to wear proper work garments and not be so easily identified as a prisoner would place him in a more advantageous position. He would still need to get a better idea of where to go once he effected his escape. That required both patience and diligence. Those he had in abundance. The only issue now was time, a decidedly unknown commodity.

As lunch ended, Schneiter tapped Eihann on the shoulder to gain his attention. Hammerschmidt was startled for a moment, a situation that concerned him. He was supposed to be in control and aware of everything around him. That capacity to be almost stoic, serene, and yet focused was the primary reason he was chosen for this mission. That and his training as an ordnance officer. A momentary lapse could be dangerous.

Schneiter motioned for Eihann to follow him, grab a tool tray and a pair of gloves. The two of them walked about a hundred yards away from the others, along a fence that bordered the farm, and to a point where the post was leaning and the barbed wire had come loose.

"Wie heißen Sie?" (What's your name?*)*

"Hammerschmidt."

"Wissen Sie, wie man Zäune befestigt?" (Do you know how to fix fences?)

Eihann nodded. He really didn't know, never having dealt with barbed wire other than stringing it along a secured battle zone. His intuition would guide him. Working quickly and efficiently, they repaired the fence in less than thirty minutes. Out of the corner of his eye, the German watched as Private Friebus kept looking back and forth between the men on the detail and him and Schneiter. This was apparently all new to him, as though he had minimal training in being a guard and never had been advised how to handle unique situations such as what presented itself now. It was obvious he did not want to be the first guard at Camp Concordia to allow a prisoner to escape or to shoot one in defense.

As the two of them walked back toward the men harvesting, Schneiter asked, "Do you speak English?"

"Little." Eihann again sounded like a child uncertain of his words. This farmer spoke German too well for him to try to communicate secretly with any other soldier.

"Are you wanting to learn?" Eihann nodded enthusiastically. "All right, no more speaking in German. We will speak in English. Yes?"

"Ja." A pause before a correction. "Yes."

At the end of the first day, Mrs. Schneiter gave each man a small loaf of brown bread and a stick of summer sausage. Speaking mostly in English as though they might understand, she indicated she wasn't sure if it would remind them too much of their home. Unaware of the food provided at the camp, she wanted them to have something substantial to eat. Like others in town, the Schneiters were skeptical, apprehensive, but also curious and desperately needing the workers. A little Christian courtesy would go a long way. Hammerschmidt knew what he had in his hands.

Schneiter leaned into the back of the truck after they loaded and said, "*Sie Männer arbeiten gut heute. Ich freue mich darauf, Sie morgen zu sehen.*" (You men worked well today. I look forward to seeing you tomorrow.)

The other four prisoners nodded in appreciation. Schneiter's gaze met Hammerschmidt's. Eihann acknowledged, stone-faced.

****

Upon his return to the camp, Boehmler and Loeher questioned him, trying to determine if they, too, wished to join a work detail.

"They're nice people," Hammerschmidt responded casually.

"Is that all you have to say?" a stunned Loeher inquired.

"Look, no matter what you do, stay here or work on a farm, you're still a prisoner. Yes?"

"Yes," Boehmler acknowledged, "but no one is shooting at you."

Hammerschmidt recognized these boys would never understand the pride of being a German soldier and what the greater cause was. He was alone on this mission, not able to confide in either the officers who were interred with him (and who were living in the lap of luxury) or these simple-minded children, as he thought of them, who were supposed to be his comrades. From now on, he would hide his feelings and work out the details necessary to continue on with his task. It would save him much needed time.

The next morning, Schneiter had Hammerschmidt chopping wood near the barn while the other members of the crew continued harvesting. Schneiter had convinced Private Friebus he could watch over the prisoner, given how agreeable they all were to the work at hand. As the whole process was new, Schneiter convinced Friebus to accept his evaluation, though he still might have been concerned about a harsh reprimand if something went wrong. Eihann stood there with a blank look while all this transpired, easily understanding what they were saying.

A pickup truck Schneiter routinely used to retrieve supplies in town had some engine issues, noticeably the starter. Once it turned over, the engine purred. He was working on it when Eihann looked up, nodding his head in the direction of the motor.

He tinkered around under the hood, using a finger swirling in the air to indicate Schneiter should start the engine. It turned over the first time. Schneiter was impressed.

"Loose. Um, how you say, *verteilerkappe*?"

"Distributor cap," Schneiter translated. Eihann nodded, a slight smile on his face.

"Where you learn German?"

"My parents were from Bavaria."

"No more Bavaria," Hammerschmidt said forcefully. "Now Germany."

"Yes, I know." Schneiter paused reflectively, a sigh escaping his lips. "I was born here. My parents continued to speak German in the house."

"That's good."

"Perhaps."

Hammerschmidt was developing a bond with the man whose farm he worked. It would have been the same under different circumstances. In this case, however, this bond would hopefully provide him with the opportunity to fulfill his assignment.

Time was always a factor. More troops would come to Camp Concordia. Even though he didn't know when exactly, he could assume it would be sooner than later. There were additional prisoners assigned to work details. Back at the camp, they spoke mostly about the hospitality of the farmers and their families, the homes with their quaintness and charm, and how these people seemed to be merely hard-working folks who earned everything by the sweat of their brow. It was unlike the propaganda they fed to them at army indoctrination. Eihann was aghast but hid it. While he understood the U.S. soldiers were following the rules of the Geneva Convention, there was nothing that said prisoners were required to love their captors or embrace their values. He, each of them for that matter, was still a German. The greatest degree of courtesy and kindness was not going to change his call to duty. Prisoner, yes, but still a German soldier. He knew his mission was even more important now.

Chapter Four

The only other person who was aware of our activities was Chief Richardson. Agents Burke and Gordon showed up at the station a few times, trying to appear as though they weren't asking questions, even though that's exactly what they were doing. There were times I had to keep from laughing in their faces. It made it more unappealing to assist them even though the end results would have been beneficial for everyone. If only they had just honestly reached out to us for assistance it all wouldn't seem like a Marx Brothers routine. I was wondering if these fellas got their training at a Saturday matinee.

After a week of diligent research, Evan Cobb had a list to go over with me. We snuck into a conference room and drew the blinds.

"There's a lot, Baron. To be honest with you, I don't know how we're going to pin it down."

"Start from the beginning."

"Well, for refineries, we've got Kanotex here and National Refining Company over in Coffeyville."

"Interesting. That's only about seventy-five miles from Tulsa."

"Roughly. Then there's Phillips and Conoco in Ponca City, which is further away."

"So maybe it's all about blowing up a refinery. You destroy property, maybe kill a few workers or someone in the community, who are all scared. But with so many refineries just in this area, what does it eventually accomplish?"

"Fear." It was something I didn't think would happen, not when there was such resolve and unity throughout the country. After all, we had experienced a surprise attack from the Japanese at Pearl Harbor. But nothing had transpired on the mainland. Most folks seemed to think the trouble was "over there." The destruction of something like a refinery in any community would have brought the war to our own back door.

"What about military bases? Hammerschmidt is supposed to be an ordnance man, right?"

"Wichita Army Airfield. Probably the biggest in the area. But there are also air bases in Independence and Coffeyville…"

"There's Coffeyville again."

"Midwest Air Depot and the Tulsa Municipal Airport."

"And Strother Army Airfield just opened here. So far, from what I'm hearing from you, Tulsa and Coffeyville as well as Ark City have viable targets."

"Well, let's say more than one. There are a lot of viable targets. Of course, I don't know much about being a saboteur."

Cobb identified each of the military groups associated with these bases in an attempt to determine if one had more importance over the other. He was right: it was a big list. There was a war on and everyone was pulling their weight. It seemed like small towns you hadn't heard of before participated in the war effort in any way they could. I couldn't fault Evan for being unable to narrow it down any more. One escaped prisoner of war in a state this size with so many targets to choose from was the proverbial needle in a haystack.

I headed on over to the office of the *Ark City Traveler* to have a conversation with Sandy Clevenger. Her title of Secretary didn't even begin to cover everything she did there. Back in '38, she helped me research horrific killings so I could guide my counterparts up in Wichita on a case involving a sadistic ripper. You couldn't tell from her silver hair and quaint demeanor how much she enjoyed digging up such dirt.

"Any time you come by," she said as soon as she saw me, "it's always something bad."

"Just here to pick your brain." I tried to sound casual. Don't know if I did.

"On what?'

"Let's say you were a talented German soldier roaming around the state of Kansas and wanted to raise a ruckus. Where do you suppose you'd go?"

"All depends on what my talent was."

"Explosives."

She whistled as though she were impressed with her imaginary skills.

"Well, just because I live in Ark City, I'd say Kanotex. Make an awfully big bang, now, wouldn't it?"

"That's what I thought. Still, what'd be the point?"

"You know, the only way folks know about this war is through the newspapers and radio and newsreels at the picture show. Some folks got kin fighting who send letters. But for the most part it doesn't seem real. You blow up something big right where they live, well, that would get everyone's attention real fast."

As I figured, Sandy saw things the way I did. With my eyes blank, I turned to leave.

"Baron," she called after me, "do we have anything to worry about?" It was the first time since I'd known her she had any fear in her eyes.

"Not as long as I'm around, dear." My smile was just like the cowboy in the white outfit just before he mounted his horse and rode off.

Marcus Hayes left Ark City at three a.m. the next morning for a nearly five-hour drive up to Concordia. Knowing him, he was probably going to disregard the chief's suggestion of staying at a lodging overnight and make the long haul back at midnight. He was the kind of guy who would do whatever it took and disregard his personal circumstances. Dave Morton kept pestering Linda Kuchenberg, the switchboard operator at the station, to call various government departments in Kansas City, Oklahoma City, Dallas, and Washington, D.C. No one seemed to have info on prisoners of war much less admit there were camps in small towns throughout the country, even though federal agents advised us of this to the contrary. Occasionally, I saw Burke and Gordon meandering around downtown trying conspicuously to be inconspicuous. I couldn't help but wonder what information they were gathering or, for that matter, what they were even doing. There weren't too many people I figured who might give those boys the time of day.

Marcus was gone longer than expected. We had no way of reaching out to him except maybe to ring the sheriff of Cloud County. We didn't want to tip our hand, so we just waited. It was important all of us maintain our active duty patrols and continue on as before. It kind of got me a little upset to run into Burke and Gordon at the Elmo, seeing as how that had now become my home, and it felt an awful lot like they were intruders, guests who hadn't been invited and decided to crash the party. Even if I had a notion to strike up a conversation, it felt like they would be close-mouthed and unresponsive. We were running into a wall at every turn, so I couldn't imagine them having any more success. Apparently, they knew something we didn't.

It didn't surprise me when Chief Richardson called me in to a meeting with the agents. Gordon's face was still stone cold, but Burke had the joviality of Fatty Arbuckle. They got around to asking for help without really asking for it. It was only a matter of time.

"We're finding that many residents are, shall we say, reluctant to talk with us," Burke said, sounding like he should work for the State Department. "I'm certain if your officers were to accompany us, we might be able to find a bit more cooperation and can get the information we need."

"You feel that way, too, Agent Gordon?" I was hoping I could get this statue of a man to at least talk.

"No, I don't. This is a federal investigation, and people have an obligation to cooperate." We stared at each other, waiting for one of us to blink. It seemed like it would have taken until the first snow on the ground for that to happen. "But I understand Agent Burke's perspective."

The air in the room was starting to heat up, steamy like a Florida afternoon in July. I caught myself with a slight smirk at my success in pulling this man's true thoughts out into the open. I saw something in his eyes that acknowledged a modest defeat, as though caving in to the local police was proving they couldn't handle such an important case. I glanced over his shoulder and saw Marcus Hayes walking by the office, continuing on when he realized the G-men were with us.

"Officers Witherspoon and Morton will be happy to accompany you and, shall we say, encourage the residents to cooperate." Chief Richardson's deep baritone voice broke the spell cast by the agent's pompous attitude. "They shouldn't have any trouble convincing our citizens of the importance of this investigation." He made it sound like folks would trust us more than them. Come to think of it, I suppose he was just being honest.

"I'll get Morton." I stood up as crisply as the crease in my pants, needing to get some fresh air and talk with Marcus. He was with Dave Morton, standing at the desk sergeant's area.

"Dave, you and I will be working with the federal agents. We might finally get a sense of this whole thing. Go to the chief's office and keep them busy for a bit while I talk with Marcus." Dave nodded and walked away briskly while Marcus and I found an empty office. He took out a notebook which appeared to have several markings inside.

"Hammerschmidt was last reported working on some machinery in John Schneiter's barn. Schneiter claimed Hammerschmidt left with the other prisoners on the return truck. When they did a head count at nine p.m., the person in Hammerschmidt's bunk was Schneiter's son. The kid claimed he was curious as to what was in the camp and that his dad was putting up the German in their house. When the soldiers got to the Schneiter's farm, he claimed he knew nothing about it and saw Hammerschmidt get on the truck. A lot of malarkey as far as I'm concerned. No one could figure anything out at that point, whether the kid or his dad was lying. By that time, it was a full five and a half hours after the trucks returned from the various farms. That would have been a heck of a head start."

"What's the story on this Schneiter fella?"

"Parents were from Bavaria. Came over to the states after Bavaria got pulled into the German empire. Lost everything because of it. Schneiter was born in 1901. Went to local schools. Didn't go to college. Inherited the family farm. Doesn't seem like he was all that 'German' to me. Seems to be pretty happy being a good old-fashioned American farmer in Kansas. I don't know. Maybe the kid is bored and hates living on a farm and wants to see some action. That's the only way I can figure it."

"You talk to the sheriff?" Marcus nodded and went back to his notebook.

"Best he figures is either one of the army guards got bribed or fooled somehow. The other possibility is Schneiter or his son had a hand in it. Can't prove anything, though. Nobody is changing their story. The army didn't figure it was much good to sweat out a fourteen-year-old kid. They'd probably scare him so bad he'd pee his pants and that's about it. Plus, they don't want to hold Schneiter for questioning because that won't set too well with the locals. They actually want the Germans working on their farms."

"Were you able to find out anything about the sister?"

"One of the guards, a Private Cleon Snodgress, recalls talking with Hammerschmidt about her. He was all proud he had a sister in the States. Snodgress thought he was trying to make himself look like he belonged in America. Girl's name is Hamer. Susan or Suzette. Guard wasn't sure." Marcus put his notebook away in his pocket and looked straight at me. "Now what?"

"We tag along with the federal boys and see what they know. In the meantime, you and Evan try to locate this Hamer gal. We need to find out what she knows about her big brother. She just might be the key to all this."

We had FBI agents who didn't want to work with us and didn't like talking to us, a missing German ordnance officer, and a whole lot of questions. The one thing I figured, the thing I could finally admit to, was Arkansas City was the bull's-eye on this target.

****

Camp Concordia—The Schneiter Farm

One by one, John Schneiter found a reason to dismiss various prisoners assigned to his work detail. Laziness, lack of cooperation, inability to do the work, no desire to learn how to do the work, bad attitude. All minor infractions but counterproductive to the reason for these work details and the need by the farmers of these laborers. Another soldier deemed more qualified replaced each, by agreement with the leadership of the camp. The only one he found no fault with was Oberfeldwebel Eihann Hammerschmidt.

In spite of the regulations against working on heavy machinery, Schneiter allowed Hammerschmidt to engage in whatever work was of primary importance to him and his farm. This was all that mattered and, in his mind, allowed him to skirt the rules. A work detail may have been a privilege for the prisoners but was a necessity to those who owned the farms. Eventually, the soldier in charge of this detail, Private Friebus, rotated out in favor of Private Cleon Snodgress. No one was ever around long enough to see Hammerschmidt almost becoming a part of the Schneiter household and the attachments he was forming with the family.

The work details started arriving earlier and staying later. Mrs. Schneiter either prepared a larger lunch or a full dinner for the crew. Eihann sat to the right of John Schneiter at the table. There was hardly any conversation outside of Schneiter making an occasional comment in German to one of the prisoners, asking them if they enjoyed the meal or inquiring as to their well-being. They seemed to appreciate someone who could speak their language; it made them feel accepted. Hammerschmidt, on the other hand, always remained quiet.

After dinner toward the end of the second week, Schneiter sat on the porch with Eihann, smoking cigarettes.

"Have you written to your family?" the farmer questioned plaintively.

"*Nicht mehr Englisch. Wir sollten Deutsch sprechen.*" (No more English. We should speak German.)

"Why?"

"*Es ist, wer du bist.*" (It is who you are.)

Eihann watched as Schneiter blew smoke in the direction of the moon. Perhaps it was toward a lost family history. Eihann recognized John Schneiter was torn between his upbringing as an American, having been born right there in Kansas, and the melancholy of what his parents were forced to give up, what he had never truly known but was now reminded of by the Germans within his community. A sense of culture and history superseded by an adoptive one he somehow could not fully embrace. He was counting on that feeling of loss in order to engage him further.

"My sister is in Tulsa," Hammerschmidt continued in English. This time it sounded more precise and refined. "She left Germany some time ago. Maybe she is happy, yes?"

"Maybe. Have you written her?" Eihann shook his head negatively. "Why not?"

"I don't want to be disappointed."

If his sister truly was happy having made a life for herself in America, he would have to come to terms with the notion she was now the enemy in his mind and in his heart. Yet it was not what he wanted to present to Schneiter if there were any possibility of enlisting his help in escaping.

"You should write her, tell her where you are. She will be pleased." Schneiter was sounding paternal, looking out for a prisoner of war he had come to consider as a kind of son. He didn't fathom the emotional investment with someone who, for the moment, was the enemy.

"After the war, we will be sent back. I will not be able to stay with her."

"True. But you could come back if you are sponsored. You could have a life here, perhaps with your sister." While he recognized Schneiter's compassionate thought, Eihann knew his life was in Germany, either as victor or vanquished. This land did not ultimately appeal to him. It lacked the sense of history *Das Vaterland,* the Fatherland, held for him. It was all he knew and all he wanted to know.

Over the next several days, Eihann roamed around the Schneiter farm appearing considerably less than a prisoner of war and more like a long-lost cousin. By this time, he was wearing dungarees with a flannel shirt and heavy work boots. Schneiter's son, Arthur, gave him a couple of red neckerchiefs. For the most part, he looked like any other itinerant farm worker passing through town. He had the appearance he needed. Now he had to turn Schneiter more fully into an ally.

During a break, Eihann and Arthur threw a baseball back and forth with gloves from the local team. Baseball was not a popular sport in Germany, but it was important to show some ease in participating with the kid. Eihann was surprised at the young man's arm strength. He also noticed, while wearing a cap, perhaps pulled down to the eyes, the two of them had more than a passing resemblance.

Eihann stopped when Schneiter was on his way to the barn.

"I wrote her," he exclaimed jubilantly. "My sister. I wrote her. I told her that one day I want to live with her in Tulsa."

Schneiter nodded but didn't seem enthused.

"What if they don't let you come back?"

"Why wouldn't they? No more war. I would not be a prisoner, just another man wanting to live in America. Yes?"

"Things are complex now, Eihann. Who knows how they will be when the war ends."

Schneiter turned to go into the barn. Eihann reached out for him, but the gesture was sudden and harsh. Schneiter turned, and Eihann pulled his hand away quickly. If Schneiter saw it as an aggressive act, it would cause the German to be dismissed from the work detail and ruin his mission.

"I cannot go back to stay." Fear and desperation filled Hammerschmidt's eyes. "A soldier. A Nazi soldier in Germany after the war ends. Do you know what will happen to me? Do you? I can't. I simply can't."

John Schneiter believed Oberfeldwebel Eihann Hammerschmidt, believed he no longer wished to be a soldier and fight, believed he wanted only to reunite with his remaining family and live a productive life here in America. He was channeling Hans Albers once again. Schneiter had been convinced he was desperate to be with his sister and fearful that would not happen after the war, whenever that may be.

"Yes. I do know."

That was what Hammerschmidt needed to hear. Schneiter had taken the bait.

That night while sitting on the porch smoking, Schneiter casually mentioned it was over three hundred miles from Concordia to Tulsa, or about four hundred and eighty kilometers; there were many farm roads between Concordia and Wichita; and Wichita was now a bustling metropolis with an influx of workers in the aircraft industry. Eihann nonchalantly asked how far it was to the Kansas-Oklahoma border; the estimation was two hundred miles, roughly three hundred and twenty kilometers. Schneiter indicated how it was a good thing to look after a man and his family but aiding and abetting a criminal was something no one should do who wasn't willing to accept the consequences.

Eihann emphasized how a man needs to follow his passions, otherwise he ceases to be a man. The two of them finished their cigarettes, never clearly stating anything yet understanding each other completely.

Chapter Five

To protect and serve. The motto of ours and just about every police department in the United States. Sometimes I wondered how we were going to get this done, especially when you considered the war in Europe and Asia and the possibility someone we knew well was working with a German saboteur. I often thought I would have to go back to thinking like a gangster, the way 'Crazy' Jake Hickey would have thought and acted. I remembered watching a movie last year, something with Humphrey Bogart about New York City gangsters going up against Nazi saboteurs. When push came to shove, even the gangsters didn't like Nazis. If there was not a lot of confidence instilled from Bogie, where would that leave me?

A German prisoner of war who escaped from a facility all the way up in Concordia was only going to impact Ark City once he got here. There were miles of roads between us and as many opportunities he could get caught or lost along the way. In the meantime, we all had our jobs to do. I took over Dave Morton's night patrol, as he had been busy all afternoon trying to locate Hammerschmidt's sister through whatever records were available, and there weren't all that many. On top of that, there were few federal agencies or departments willing to cooperate. My mind wandered, and my feet shuffled along, carrying me somewhere to the outskirts of town. Too much thinking had left my mind fogged over. Before I knew it, I was down by the Arkansas River. My breathing grew faster when I realized I was at the spot where Natalie Dixon ended her vengeful quest along with her life eight years prior. My heart nearly stopped when I saw a figure standing in the exact spot she had been.

He wore a brown long-sleeved shirt, soiled tan work pants, and heavy boots. There was a red kerchief tied around his neck and something resembling a train conductor's hat pulled down and covering his eyes. For all the appearance of ruggedness, this was a frail man. Abram Dutcher had lost the elegance that made him a figure of authority, a man I had come to respect for his honesty and straightforward attitude. He still, however, retained his dignity.

Dutcher controlled all the crime activities in southern Kansas and parts of Oklahoma and Missouri at the turn of the century but was forced out by the local politicians about the time of the Great War. 'Der Kaiser', as he was respectfully known, hid underground and still had a hand in much of what went on but saw none of the glory. Perhaps power was only an illusion. While he may have been instrumental in guiding me with the capture of Jake Hickey, he had pretty much become a ghost whose whereabouts were known only to Karla Frankl and the few trusted confidantes who remained from those days of old. His time had long passed, but his importance to me was still just as great.

I crossed the river at a low point, my shoes getting slightly wet. It was strange to me Dutcher would have been standing in the exact spot where I last saw Natalie alive. Maybe he knew somehow. Then I realized it wasn't a maybe.

"These are tough times we are in." His voice still retained its eloquence, like an esteemed professor or a mesmerist.

"The question is: Am I talking to an enemy of America?"

His laugh was breathless and strained.

"Even I am considered an enemy of the German government, Officer Witherspoon. And my influence here is very nearly obsolete, as you are certainly aware."

"Where would an escaped prisoner of war go in Kansas? Try to make it back to Germany?"

"Not the homeland or the theaters of war. Remember: He is still a soldier. He still has a mission."

"What mission?"

"Chaos. Mayhem. Forcing you to use your valuable resources and time to recapture one lone man. He can create a good deal of havoc just by running and hiding. He does not really have to do much else. You will do all of his work for him."

"I've got two federal agents milling about. It must be something more."

Dutcher removed his cap, undid his kerchief, and wiped his head with it. It was a cool evening, but he looked like he had been sweating profusely. A harsh cough followed. He doubled over and covered his mouth. As he straightened up, I saw bloody phlegm on the kerchief.

"Americans believe Germans go to war on a particular day, after it has been declared by their government. The truth is they prepare for it for many years. Even though you got into the Great War late,

Wilhelm had sent many English-speaking agents over here years in advance. Many were simply liaisons for the actual saboteurs who he believed would be smuggled in."

"So the prisoner who is on the loose, he is a saboteur?"

"What was his position?"

"Ordnance."

Dutcher nodded, his eyebrow raised in validation.

"And you're saying there is probably some kind of agent here to meet him, guide him as it were?"

"That is the way it was done in the past. As you know, Hitler is a student of history. Besides, he is even more devious than Wilhelm ever could be."

It all made sense, but there were still too many pieces missing. Dutcher coughed again, fell to one knee, and then stood as though what I witnessed was only in my imagination. Out of respect, I acted accordingly.

"Are you all right?"

"I am dying, Baron. This may be the last time we meet."

I thought of Doctor Brenz and the hospital and so many different things. It occurred to me this man, though he had been head of a large criminal empire, had a kind of decency and a code of honor rarely seen in men that are more reputable. He turned to walk away, perhaps forever.

"How did you pick this spot?" I called back to him.

"I watched your pain that day. I hoped it would diminish. I am glad to see it has in some measure." A small charming smile appeared on his face. "Now, however, it is time to focus on larger matters that exceed both your life and mine." Within a matter of a moment, he was gone. I knew it would be forever.

There was a small part of me that wished to reminisce. About Eric Kimble, the tough from the North Side of Chicago. About Baron Witherspoon, the fallen war hero whose name would live on. About Jake Hickey and Heather Devore and Natalie Dixon and Ronnie Roché, and Eliot Ness. The long journey hadn't yet ended. There was a war being waged. The memories would always be there. I had to bring my mind back to today.

I slept very little after my shift as notions churned in my mind much in the same way they had when I was contemplating the identities of murderers from years ago. It was apparent Eihan Hammerschmidt had a secondary mission of sabotage as well as a contact near where the event would take place. The realization struck me the FBI agents knew this was probably going on all over the country and were quietly trying to stop anything before it happened. It was time to put our cards on the table.

It wasn't my intention to barge into Chief Richardson's office. He had come to expect it from me when a wild idea swirled around in my head. As he had agents Burke and Gordon with him, it did seem a tad unprofessional of me. However, I figured we could throw the niceties of professionalism out the window in this instance. I wanted the truth and was going to get it.

"So do you think an ordnance man is going to try to get back to Germany?" I rambled.

"No." It was the first time Gordon spoke up before Burke. "We have intelligence to indicate these escapees—"

"These escapees? I thought we were talking about Hammerschmidt."

"Officer Witherspoon, this is not the first case of a German prisoner of war escaping from a rural camp." While Burke's tone was soothing, the underlying comment was disturbing. There was an air of menace permeating the room. I looked over to the chief and then back to Burke.

"These various escapees have secondary targets." Gordon continued as though there had been no interruption. "A tank gunner from the Afrika Corps escaped from Camp Ashby and was picked up not too far from Norfolk, Virginia, about forty miles from the naval station there. Another member of the Afrika Corps went missing from Camp Clinton. Many of the generals housed there kept lying about his whereabouts for close to three weeks before he was finally picked up near the train station in Jackson, Mississippi, less than four miles from the Adjutant General's office."

"You see, Officer Witherspoon," Burke softly said, sounding like one of those psychiatrists who make you lie on a couch and tell your life story, "there's been a pattern of Afrika Corps soldiers escaping from prison camps and winding up near something that could be considered a possible target. Camp Concordia housed men from the Afrika Corps. Given what has previously transpired, we are simply not willing to leave anything to chance."

"Any of these soldiers have any affiliation with the U.S., any knowledge of the area?"

The two agents looked at each other as though it were a trick question.

"No." Gordon returned to his brusque responses.

"How far were these other POW camps from where the soldiers were eventually picked up?"

Burke checked his ever-present notebook.

"Both were about ten to twelve miles away."

"But you've got this Hammerschmidt guy coming all the way down some two hundred miles just to blow up something in little old Arkansas City? How do you suppose he's going to carry out any kind of sabotage without any weapons or explosives or safe havens along the way?"

"What are you getting at, Witherspoon?" I was starting to get under Gordon's skin.

"If these escaped prisoners were intent upon sabotage, they would need some kind of assistance or guidance. Certainly within a ten-mile spread but most definitely for as far away as Hammerschmidt is traveling."

"There are many Nazi sympathizers here in the States," Gordon continued with a sense of boredom, "many of whom are intent upon—"

I shook my head aggressively.

"Look, I'm familiar with the Duquesne Spy Ring." It was a good thing I had spoken to Sandy Clevenger, she being my best source for research and information throughout the years. "We're not talking about a group of people who have been hunkered down in the U.S. for years waiting for their opportunities. You've got escaped prisoners of war. They're not just going to randomly walk up to someone who looks German and ask for help. And your boy from Camp Concordia is not going on a long journey hoping to find someone who is sympathetic to his cause. Those other guys were within a day's hike from those camps."

"What's your point?" Gordon continued with his boredom, but I noticed Burke's eyes glazed over with interest. Chief Richardson let me ride this pony all the way to the finish line.

"Why don't we assume for a moment Hitler's plan for world conquest caused him to fashion a program of internal agents, living here and fitting into various communities, all of which were located near something worthy of sabotage. Select soldiers had a list of camps and targets and contacts to memorize. The intent was to have the soldier find the contact and carry out a designated mission."

"Tend to read a lot of *Black Mask* stories, Officer Witherspoon?" Agent Gordon was doing his best to dismiss any theory put forth by what he more than likely considered to be a backwoods hick. If only he knew.

"You guys are looking for the soldier. You need to be looking for his contact." I realized my comments put me in agreement with the agents, who made such assumptions earlier but without any viable connection to the case. Their conjecture without any facts raised the hair on the back of my neck. I had just made it clear and out in the open, a theory with some teeth in it.

There was a moment, maybe less than thirty seconds, of complete silence. The beat cops and night patrol officers were not supposed to be coming up with the answers to complex issues. Back when the FBI was a ragtag group of untrained college boys, you could expect a bit of disorganization. It was hard to believe Burke and Gordon were here for as long as they had been and yet did not seem to make any progress. Not that my declaration was going to course through their bodies like electricity to a condemned man, but at the very least, I thought they might respond positively. Heck, I thought they would simply respond.

I looked at the chief and nodded in a professional and respectful manner, then turned to leave. It wasn't certain whether the federal agents were seeking success or glory. To my way of thinking, I didn't think they would find either.

Chapter Six

Chief Richardson knew how important it was for us to be diligent with our research but also recognized we were a police department and tasked with law enforcement beyond the happenings of the war a long way outside of our jurisdiction. As such, he assigned me and Evan Cobb to review a series of armed robberies all around south central Kansas. The possibility existed the bandit might try to strike somewhere in Ark City. An unidentified assailant, his face covered by a handkerchief, had held up various businesses in Harper, Caldwell, Wellington, and Winfield. Seemed a little like a bandit from the 1920's in Arizona or New Mexico to me. Reports indicated he was dressed in a tan suit with white shirt and red tie and brown-and-white saddle shoes. While he might have had a fashion sense, the total take from the four robberies only came to a little over $2500. Dillinger would have sneezed at that.

The primary reason we surmised he could be heading in our direction was due to the unlikely prospect this almost certain amateur wouldn't try his hand up in Wichita. I think he would annoy the police up there. We sent a report out to all patrolmen based on the description given. I didn't recognize the gray Plymouth Coupé, '38 or '39, which drove through town, nor could I make out the driver's face, but it seemed awfully like the shared report. Perhaps I was on edge with the war and the FBI men and this darned fool running around. It was just that we didn't get a whole lot of new people coming into Ark City. I had the choice of following the car and potentially make an innocent man feel awkward or let it go about its business, hoping its business was at least something legal.

My shift ended at four in the afternoon. I was making my way back toward the station when I heard a woman scream from a block over and then a gunshot. As I approached the intersection of Summit and Vine, Cobb ran down north from Summit. We saw the car and the guy at the same time, parked out in front of Brady Mercantile. He was shooting back toward the store. The owner, Thomas Brady, was a feisty old coot who didn't cotton to anyone imposing upon him in any regard, even if they did have a gun. He'd never been in the military, but he sure held his ground like a soldier.

"Police!" I yelled. The guy turned toward me and fired an errant shot. I returned fire twice, and Cobb got off a couple of rounds. It wasn't our intention to kill him but that's how it wound up whether we liked it or not. There were likely a few towns grateful they didn't have to spend the time or the money on a trial.

I went through the guy's personal effects while Dr. Brenz performed a cursory autopsy. This would be largely for the extensive amount of paperwork required when one criminal died in the commission of a crime. I had been through this routine numerous times with Brenz, and neither of us seemed rattled by dead bodies.

"Joshua Warshaw," I said aloud, reading the driver's license. "He's from Pueblo, Colorado. I wonder if he worked for the Carlino brothers." I looked down at him wondering if guys from Colorado looked a particular way different from guys in Kansas.

"Who was he?" Doctie asked.

"Well, he certainly was no Jake Hickey." He was a thorn in my side when we were young and a threat after I had long settled in here. Then again, it was Big Ray Vernon, a former Ark City policeman and now high school basketball coach, who could take credit for that one.

I sat at my desk filling out the reports when it occurred to me this was the first person I'd killed since the war. It might have been easy to believe it was both Cobb and me. But I knew I hit him once in the heart and once in the belly. I wasn't scared or flustered or dismayed. Nothing. The truly disturbing thing was I realized I could kill someone and not feel anything. Was that part of the job or part of me? It was best not to consider the answer further.

I walked home in a bit of a fog when Alex Gordon approached me outside the Elmo. There was nothing apologetic or sociable about him, and it wasn't like he was trying to make up for being a sour apple. It was simply business he was carrying on with and seemed to expect me to do the same. He had a list of various people who had recently arrived in Arkansas City within the last five years. The indication was the list might have been longer if he went back ten years on account of the people looking for jobs at the mills or refineries while the Depression was going on. I was really too tired to give him my full attention but was grateful he had thought enough of me to ask. Perhaps I was giving him more credit than he was due.

We stood in the lobby as I looked over his three-page typed list. He kept looking around, over his shoulder and off to the side, as though we were in the middle of planning some kind of crime. I caught his hesitance out of the corner of my eye but had to decide between helping him out and being completely put off by him. I reckoned I would try both. Some names were familiar, but a whole lot didn't ring a bell. That wasn't such a bad thing for a cop. If I knew you, it was either because I saw you a lot around town or you might be a criminal. Unfamiliar names took on a whole new meaning in the world we were living in now.

"Agent Gordon—"

"Alex." I was actually quite surprised at him turning out to be human after all.

"Alex, do you mind if I take this to my room and peruse it up there? I really need to get off my feet. You know, the life of a beat cop."

He nodded begrudgingly. I started to go upstairs, and then turned back.

"Do federal agents drink?" I asked.

"More than you know." It was the first time I'd seen him smile. More human than I gave him credit for.

A bottle of hooch and a couple of glasses was on top of my dresser alongside my comb and brush. I poured a snort for the two of us and swallowed mine quickly. Some of it seemed to have caught in his throat and he coughed once or twice.

"There's a guy lives halfway between here and Winfield. He has a still from back when. Never gave up even after Prohibition ended. Makes a fine corn mash."

"Tastes like North Side bathtub gin."

It caught me off guard to hear him say that,

although I made sure to keep my face as cold as stone. I had thought he and Burke were from Washington, D.C. It might have been he had done some time up there in a field office. He seemed like he was too young to have been around back then, but it was my mistake not to pay more attention to the two of these federal agents than I had. There was no sense inquiring any further. Over twenty years had passed since I had left Eric Kimble and the North Side gang behind. I went back to looking at his list.

"Off hand, there are half a dozen guys who may be newer to town, but they've been upright citizens. James McDonald works at Kanotex, but he came up from another refinery in Texas. Good old boy who likes to chat your ear off. Ralph Houseman is a handyman for Dixie at Daisy Mae's. Reggie Littlejohn is over at Le Stourgeon packing plant. Pretty quiet guy for the most part. Church-going fella."

"It doesn't mean all that much if you think about it. The thing is whoever the contact is fits in, looks like everyone else, acts like everyone else. He's not an outsider in terms of appearances. He is a 'good old boy' or a 'handyman' or 'a church-going fella' because he can't be seen as anything else."

I understood what he was getting at, but it still didn't seem to make much sense the Nazis would have planted any of those guys or others here to work quiet, meaningless lives for several years waiting for an opportunity to strike. Then again, I didn't know much about espionage or Nazis. Gordon nodded and started to leave after finishing his drink.

"Shame you're the only place in town that offers a decent drink." His hand was on the doorknob and his back was to me.

"Well, you've got to know where to look, Alex."

He nodded and left. I wasn't too sure, but there might have been another smile on his face.

A few minutes later there was a knock at my door. I figured Gordon was coming back. It was Carl Pearson, the night man at the Elmo. Carl was mostly quiet but could throw in a zinger just to catch your attention. He was holding an envelope.

"Hey, Baron, Dave Morton left this for you. But I seen you with that G-man so I didn't want to interrupt you."

"No worries, Carl. Say, how have them federal boys been?"

"Quiet. Hardly see 'em coming or going. Scares me a bit."

"They been asking for anything?"

"Nothing special. Every once in a while they ask some kind of question about somebody or other. It ain't pointing any fingers but more like asking me what I think about them. Strikes me as pretty odd."

I nodded and thanked him. Seems like the FBI was grasping at straws.

The note inside was simple: We found her. Looks like we're heading down to Tulsa.

****

Camp Concordia—The Planning

Eihann made it known to anyone who would listen how much he loved his sister, how proud he was of her, and how much he knew it was the right thing to go live with her after the war. She was right, he proclaimed, to have left Germany when she did, knowing there would be only misery for her if she stayed. He asked anyone who would answer what they knew about the city of Tulsa in the state of Oklahoma, what kind of a life he might have there, and if they would make fun of him and his German accent. What kind of job he could get. How it would be there for a former German soldier. How life, in general, would be so much better in America. Yes, Tulsa, Oklahoma and his beloved sister was the answer to his future.

Tulsa. His sister. He kept repeating those two things like the lyrics to a song. Anyone remembering would head in that direction. They wouldn't expect him anywhere else. It was the conscious effort of a deliberate plan. The truth was Eihann Hammerschmidt hardly remembered his sister, barely thought about her as a person, much less a member of his family. She left because being German was an embarrassment to her. If he had a choice in the matter, she would have been a target as well. Her death, however, would mean nothing to the glorious war effort.

Eihann made it appear to John Schneiter he was working harder, more diligently, craving the work. Perhaps he was trying to take his mind off what Schneiter could only assume was a profound sadness. During a break while he worked on a tractor engine, Schneiter asked, "What's bothering you?"

"She is no longer a Hammerschmidt." Schneiter did not grasp the comment. "She changed her name to Hamer. It means she does not want to be part of the family, of my family." Was there perhaps a tear in Eihann's eye? The look of profound and frustrated sadness was overwhelming.

"Many people changed their name when they came here. To sound more American. It was only natural."

"You didn't. Your parents didn't." Schneiter nodded in agreement. "I don't know if she would even accept me anymore. Why would she? She lives the life of an American woman." He looked away in disgrace.

"She will accept you. You are her blood kin."

Eihann returned to working on the engine, burying his head under the hood. He was trying to disappear from the hurt and pain and desperation he felt. It was the marvelous pretense he created.

Oberfeldwebel Hammerschmidt was emerging from the solitary and uncertain cocoon he maintained upon his arrival at the camp. He reached out to younger soldiers, ensuring their safety and comfort. He liaised with officers to pass along comments and suggestions. He was friendly with the camp guards. He spoke warmly of his sister and his continued desire to reach out to her. Perhaps when his letter allowance came around he would write to her. This and this alone would provide him with some much needed hope, something to cling to in order to survive the long hours and days. It would be the thing anyone would remember about him the most.

In the meantime, he calculated a method of getting away and planning his journey to his designated destination.

Hammerschmidt, being the only prisoner to work consistently on the Schneiter farm, was accepted into the home during lunch breaks. The others, all relatively new or on their second detail, were content to stay outside in the fresh air and eat meat sandwiches and drink cool lemonade. Eihann got a hot meal, drank coffee, and smoked cigarettes on the porch where no one else could see.

It had been barely two weeks but his comfort level with the family had grown to a point where he allowed what they believed were his true feelings to emerge.

"I must see her. I cannot wait until the end of the war." He vaguely realized he spoke with not a trace of a German accent. He hoped Schneiter would attribute that to him being a quick learner. "If there is to be any hope for me, I must know now."

Schneiter had the intense look of a college professor evaluating a graduate student's thesis. He had come to know Oberfeldwebel Eihann Hammerschmidt as a diligent worker, an intelligent man, and a passionate soldier who had recognized his avocation might soon be useless.

"*Ich kann dir nicht helfen zu entkommen.*" (I cannot help you escape.)

"*Ich frage nur, dass Sie mich zur County-Linie fahren.*" (All I ask is that you drive me to the county line.)

"*Die Wache wird wissen, dass sie verschwunden bist.*" (The guard will know you have disappeared.)

Hammerschmidt smiled.

"*Ah, aber dein Sohn sieht mir so ähnlich.*" (Ah, but your son looks so much like me.)

With a precision of explanation, Hammerschmidt outlined a simple scenario: Eihann would exchange clothes with Arthur, who would wear a hat to cover as much of his face as possible. Schneiter would have "Eihann" working in the barn, sequestered from the other prisoners while at the same time assuring the guard everything was fine. Schneiter would then drive Hammerschmidt south out of town, taking farm roads to avoid driving directly through the city. At a point just north of the county line, Eihann would get out and leave, fending for himself. Schneiter would create a diversion when the detail was ready to head back to the camp. If it worked, no one would notice the disappearance until bed check. If there were any questions, he would convince the guard to allow him to drive "Eihann" back in a little bit after completing an "important task." Or, perhaps, intrigued by life in the camp, Arthur wished to know more about the German soldiers he befriended. In either case, Hammerschmidt would have a solid five- to eight-hour head start. It was risky, but the entire nature of the mission (in fact the mission of all such designated soldiers) was to fabricate the means to carry out their directive. An obvious escape would cut each mission short well before it had a chance to begin.

****

Schneiter's heart raced. Part of him knew this was tantamount to being a traitor to his country. The devout man who went faithfully to Northside Baptist Church on Sunday, however, felt this was a righteous cause that far surpassed nations and politics and war. That upright and moral man was who he needed to be. Whether it was the truth or something he convinced himself of, it wound up being the direction he would take.

****

There was never a consideration for this farmer's feelings or the repercussions of his actions. Oberfeldwebel Eihann Hammerschmidt was a soldier in the German army, still, despite being in a POW camp in Kansas of the United States. He had been one of the few chosen for a sabotage mission in the event of his capture. He rigorously memorized locations of targets in selected states, and was advised there would be a contact providing additional assistance in these various locations. These were men and women sent to America years before and had integrated themselves into communities, appearing as harmless and inconsequential workers, waiting for the opportunities to present themselves. This was the ultimate goal.

These plans were flawed and Hammerschmidt knew it. There could be no prior communication with these unidentified contacts and no verifiable way of determining who they might be. He would not know if they still lived in these towns, were alive, and not incarcerated for some other offense. The entire plan had its basis on the ability to escape from or walk away from these camps and these contacts still being available to assist in a greater cause. Barring that, these selected men were destined to pass the time until the war ended in what some might consider reasonable comfort. It was an unappealing consideration for a soldier who still believed in the cause.

Based on the information he had been able to acquire surreptitiously, Eihann calculated the distance to his target to be slightly over 321 kilometers. A loaded march would be 21 kilometers in three hours, assuming the total load with rifle at just over 30 kilograms. However, traveling light with the few tools he had secreted should increase the distance dramatically while cutting down on the fatigue factor. Based on a twelve-hour hiking day with increased distance, he figured it would take two and a half days.

This was all the more reason why he needed Schneiter to get him to at least the county line to cut down on some of the miles. Perhaps hitchhiking, a ride here and there, would decrease the time even further. Assuming he didn't get bogged down or stopped in a bigger city like Wichita, or by a policeman questioning an unidentified man at any point along the way. Too many factors; too many possibilities. None of which he would consider as they impacted the ultimate success. If there were obstacles that prevented his acquisition of the target, it would either cause delay or failure.

The mission was a priority.

But it seemed to be over before it could even get started. Schneiter started to avoid him in the later part of the afternoon, did not seem as gregarious and forthcoming, and certainly did not come across as "Christian" as he had been. Eihann knew the man was having a crisis of conscience, could feel it in his own bones. He could not afford that or allow it. There were two ways to play it: more stern or more tears. Eihann would rely on his meager acting skills again.

This time there were actual tears. Where they came from Eihann was uncertain. In the end it worked. The plan would be in effect tomorrow. Shortly after arrival to the camp.

That evening he quietly collected the few tools he had hidden. He could acquire more along the way, depending on what assistance he might actually get. The High Command had chosen him largely because his knowledge and creative approach to explosive devices exceeded his skills as an ordnance officer. He had an innate ability to manufacture something that could initiate a destructive force from basic ingredients. Having the skills necessary to improvise such a device made him an invaluable asset.

His conversations with fellow soldiers and guards

that evening were the same banality: his love for his sister; his appreciation of the fair treatment received from the American soldiers; his desire for the war to end expediently so he could go on with his life. An internal smile reminded him he would miss this theatricality. Perhaps he would use it again on the long road to his destination.

Chapter Seven

Tulsa was a good three-hour drive from Ark City. I was pleasantly surprised to see Dave Morton at the municipal building at six a.m., figuring he was still young enough to enjoy a lengthy social evening with the ladies every now and again. His eagerness on this case bode well for any future advancement he might seek within the department. After all, he had the same kind of good-natured yet hard-working attitude George McAllister had. That is, until George found it was easier to get bought out by Jake Hickey. In spite of that, I still believe we lost a good man that day.

We were mostly silent on the drive down, the cool morning air giving way to the warmth of the sun. Neither of us was much into aimless chit-chat, passing the time talking about the weather or some local gossip. We were focused on our jobs above all else. Dave drove, and I read the report he created based on info both he and Marcus were able to get from the Tulsa police and the county's registrars. The phone company, unfortunately, had been of no help at all. Something to do with privacy laws or some such thing. It didn't really matter much. After all was said and done, the truth was going to come out.

Suzanne Hamer worked for a seamstress, lived in Tulsa since she was a young girl, and was a registered Republican. She had lodged in a rooming house for nearly ten years, was not known to have any gentlemen callers, and had no record of any kind. From all we gathered, she was a quiet and almost lonely young woman. There was a part of me willing to accept the report. The other part figured she was the type a saboteur would need to make an explosive impact, someone who might have been sent ahead to lay the groundwork for something devilish and unspeakable.

The Tulsa Police Department were advised of our visit and offered us the opportunity to question her without their presence as a courtesy after both of our chiefs consulted on this matter by phone. It was an allowance made largely due to the possibility of relating to the war and an attack within either one of our cities. In any other case, there would have been puffed chests and hard talk, the kind I would have expected from Detective John Rackler up in Wichita.

"How do you want to handle it?" Dave finally spoke when we were just outside the city limits.

"I really don't want to go into this assuming she is a spy or a saboteur."

"Why? Just because she's a woman?"

"Let's just say I'd like to give everyone the benefit of the doubt. Women included."

He accepted the comment largely because it was coming from me. To Dave, everyone was guilty until proven innocent. There were few he was willing to trust, and it took some time to get to that point. When you added in spies and saboteurs, his concern was duly noted.

Carrie T's Tailoring and Alterations was on 5th Street around the corner from Main. The sign was a big white board with painted black lettering in an elegant font, yet simple and unadorned. The immediate area just inside the doorway had racks of clothing and a small counter. I assumed they did their work in a larger back room we were as yet unable to see. Carrie T herself greeted us as we entered, acknowledged we were the "men from Kansas," and led us to a small office to wait while she brought in Suzanne Hamer. The namesake of the store looked more like a farmer's wife, soft lines at the edge of her eyes and hands that looked as though they had been in constant use for a number of years. Her attitude did not let on to the weariness of such a life. We sat in uncomfortable wooden chairs in front of a plain desk, holding our hats in our hands like schoolboys waiting on a date. This was supposed to be an inquiry and not an interrogation.

Miss Hamer was petite, barely five feet, with striking red hair and green eyes. She reminded me of a down-home Oklahoma version of Maureen O'Hara but decidedly demure and certainly not outspoken. There didn't appear to be anything you could call German about her. Her gaze remained down, and she sat in the chair Dave was in once he stood up.

"I suppose you are here about my brother." The surprising ease with which she made the statement gave away the fact there was a strength hiding behind the outward shyness. Perhaps that was a strength in itself.

"Yes, ma'am. When was the last you heard from him?"

"Got a letter from him last month from the camp up in Kansas. That where you're from?"

"No, that's Concordia, about two hundred miles north of us. We got some FBI men who think he may be heading to our town, Arkansas City. You heard of it?"

"Just near the border, right?"

"Yes, ma'am. Just about."

"Why would he be going there?" She squinted in confusion, all of this war and spy stuff more than she could grasp. As she knew little about where we were from, nothing about my suggestion made any sense.

"Sabotage." Dave blurted it out a little too strong for my taste. Maybe he wasn't buying the innocence he thought she was selling or just wanted to get the answers a bit more quickly, time being of the essence. It was Dave's one major glaring flaw, an impatience that didn't allow things to simply work themselves out on their own.

He continued on with his train of thought. "Well, your brother is an ordnance man. For him to just up and leave a cozy place like Camp Concordia—"

"You call a prisoner of war camp a cozy place?" Her tone was now equal to Dave's.

"Compared to the stench of death in battle, I'd say it was a lot more cozy. They get treated a darn sight better than what our boys have to deal with over there." This was sounding more like a few domestic disputes I'd had to handle over the years, with Dave playing the part of the angry husband. Whereas I didn't think this was the best approach to take, I let it go on for a bit, hoping it would work to our advantage.

"Miss Hamer, had you received other letters from Eihan before he was captured?"

She glared at Dave before turning to me. Her tone subsided somewhat, but she didn't appreciate the notion this was now an interrogation.

"He had written throughout the war. The letters

always took long to get to me and were usually opened up by the time I got them." She might have understood the reason but resented it nevertheless.

"What were they about, I mean, if you don't mind telling me?" I recognized I was being soft-hearted in the middle of investigating a possible saboteur. So much had changed in me over the years, like trying to find the good in people before judging them. I wasn't sure if I was putting myself in danger with such an attitude. At this point we had to try everything possible to get answers. Our city had been designated a target by the FBI, and I was not going to let that happen.

"The first ones were largely about his daily life in the war. They started off with pride at being a German soldier, how much he had learned, how valued he was by his commanding officers. Then he started to grow weary and tired, said how fortunate it was I didn't go through it, and I was safer and probably happier living where I was."

"Did it sound like he wanted to get out?"

She was quiet for a moment, eyes fixed on the blank wall in front of her, not really looking at anything, but seeing something we could not see.

"Yes. Yes, I think so."

"So if he was happy to have been caught, why do you suppose he just walked away from the camp?" Dave didn't sound as nasty, but he was still pressing for real answers.

"Even a songbird grows tired of a cage." She was staring at Dave now, using all her strength and courage to push him back from her.

Carrie T was kind enough to allow us to escort Miss Hamer to retrieve the letters she'd received from her brother for the last several years. I didn't bother asking if the bundle was all of them because it wouldn't have done any good. We drove her back to work; my departing comment was meant to be diplomatic, but I feared she didn't see us as any different from the Nazis.

"We appreciate everything you've done for us. We hope we can count on you if the need arises." My heart was in it, but I am certain my tone was less than encouraging.

I let Dave drive back while I read the letters as chronologically as I could. As she had stated, many of the earlier ones were of the drudgery and life of a soldier, complaints about the lack of amenities available to them, but boasting of strength and courage. Closer to the time of capture in North Africa, there was a kind of sadness, a regret the total effort seemed wasted, and despair at what would become of Germany. His praise for his sister's situation living in America sounded a bit hopeful. It was somewhat in keeping with the information Marcus got from the prison guards that Hammerschmidt was all right with the thought of being in America. There was something that just didn't quite fit together.

"You buy her story?" Dave asked, a bit of spite in his voice.

"Hers, yes. His, no. If war is hell and the cause is lost and America is so great, why did he just walk away from Camp Concordia?"

"Exactly."

"She's been away from everything associated with Germany for a long time. She has no idea who her brother really is and what he intends to do. It would be quite easy for him to convince her he had enough and

74

was willing to change. For that matter, would she even recognize him?"

"We don't know what he intends to do, either," Dave responded, sounding defeated. "He might even try to convince her to help him somehow."

I continued reading the letters, trying in my mind to be a code breaker of some sort, and read between the lines. In the past, my devotion to Natalie Dixon betrayed me. Whereas I did not feel the same toward Suzanne Hamer, I realized how important it was to separate emotion from rational thinking.

"Hammerschmidt could have waited out the war in relative comfort and then joined his sister. Escaping from a prisoner of war camp now makes no sense unless he is involved in some kind of plot. It stands to reason."

"So assuming the Hamer girl is just a younger sister trying to reconnect with what she assumes to be a devoted older brother," Dave interjected, "there has got to be another contact in or around Ark City."

Dave's comment was the rational thinking that we needed. It was also a scary thought, considering we had absolutely no idea who that could be. Once again, it would be like walking around town blindfolded.

Chapter Eight

Daisy Mae's became our secondary meeting location. As busy as it could be at times, there was a certain degree of privacy. When you're hunkered down in a conference room in the station, it appears a tad too obvious. However, no one thought much of four policemen having lunch. Even Marcus couldn't refrain from devouring a bowl of chili or a club sandwich just like Dave, who was a notoriously loud eater. Ralph Houseman seemed to be waiting tables more than bussing them. After all these years, he had become a true asset to Dixie.

"The FBI guys seem to think someone who has been here for a while is Hammerschmidt's contact." I went into detail about the passing conversations I had when encountering them at the Elmo.

"Hey, I know this is going to sound strange," Evan interjected, "but isn't it all circumstantial that Hammerschmidt is a saboteur?"

"Come on, Cobb," Dave mumbled with a mouthful of food. "An ordnance man just walking away from a place he might call home in the future? What else would he be up to?"

"No, I get all that. But, just for argument," Evan continued, "what if he actually is trying to make his way to Tulsa to be with his sister? Maybe wait out the war there in hiding? You said she didn't appear as forthcoming as you would have preferred. So if that was his plan after all, she would be harboring a fugitive and could get in big trouble. Naturally, you kind of understand why she wouldn't be jumping up and down and admitting everything. I know it doesn't make a lot of sense, but it could."

Shaking his head and squeezing his eyes until he had almost shut them, Marcus responded, "A guy with that kind of smarts knows he'd be a fugitive as well as risking his sister's life." He had a point. "Now, she, on the other hand, might think he's coming down her way but it's entirely doubtful."

"While he may have other motives, we have to assume he is on a mission of sabotage of some kind," I continued, agreeing with Marcus. I recognized other possibilities existed, but we had to prepare for the worst case. We were policemen. That's what we did. We would leave the fairy tales to writers.

The federal agents based their list on supposition and hearsay and possibly whatever files or documents they had access to that we didn't know about. We tried to come up with names of men and women who had not been lifelong residents, who were true outsiders, but who had also blended into the fabric of daily life. Since none of us had a background for this kind of stuff, every name became like a balloon getting popped. It was truly difficult to imagine anyone we knew, from Richard Hockenberg, the filling station attendant, to Ralph Houseman, our favorite employee at Daisy Mae's, could be involved with the German war effort. I realized we were ill equipped for this, and we might have to eventually rely on Burke and Gordon. This was assuming they would allow us into their inner circle.

"What now?" I never would have expected to hear Evan Cobb sound as overwhelmed as he did. His intellect was such he always enjoyed a jigsaw puzzle or a direct challenge. I couldn't fault him for the attitude. It was an important thing we were doing, preparing for the possibility of a vicious attack somewhere in or around Ark City as part of the enemy's plan to undermine our country and its war effort. However, the fuse we lit had fizzled out. We were back to being patrol cops, realizing we were not seasoned investigators. Even after all the deduction I did back in '35 and '38, I felt more and more like I was behind the eight ball.

On a whim, I contacted Detective John Rackler at the Wichita Police Department. Rackler and his retired partner, Charlie Sells, were forced to work with me on a series of murders in their city back in '38. Neither of them requested my presence, figuring they could solve those heinous crimes on their own. When it all turned out to be a political ploy, they were happy to see me go. However, as the crimes continued, they called me back to assist. While we finally closed the case, their embarrassment at my success didn't go over too well.

"Hey, chum," Rackler intoned like Enrico Caruso with far less talent and a more rasping voice. I couldn't tell if everything in the past was all water under the bridge or if he was just humoring me with a pretense of friendship. After five years on top of becoming a full detective, I figured it didn't matter to him one way or another. Just as before, I was nothing more than the fly in the ointment.

We chatted for a bit, about the war, the many cases he had solved since I'd last seen him, and the passing of

Sells right after the start of the war, in early 1942. I was truly saddened to hear that, largely because Charlie Sells always tried to do the right thing and never got the rewards he deserved. All Rackler could talk about was how cold it was on the day of the funeral.

The conversation then drifted to the war. He told some kind of story about his rejection from the draft board, the likes of which sounded like the same bluster he had in the past. I determined it was necessary to tell him some of what was going on down here in order to get any information from him, hoping he would be professional enough to share in the name of national security. Assuming that was more important than his pride or reputation.

"All things being equal, John, I think it's more likely for something to happen in Wichita than here." I nearly choked on my own spit calling him by his first name like we were old buddies. "You've got the air base and all those manufacturing plants. Would sure make headlines, you know?"

"No way any sabotage could happen here. Chief Jaycox and Mayor Moriarty beefed up the force by hiring a lot of new guys who didn't get drafted as well as bringing back some of our veteran guys who had retired. The chief told me I'd be training those guys. You know, get them battle ready. Plus, we got a slew of our own federal agents keeping an eye on the Wichita Army Airfield as well as all those refineries out in El Dorado. Let 'em try. That's what I say. We're ready for 'em."

He made it sound like Wichita was a fortress through which no danger could pass. Either that or he was the quarterback on the college team ready for the big game. I knew from years past his confidence was all about a sense of his own importance and not on anything substantial. There were a lot of gangsters back in Chicago in the '20s who were that way as well, and none of them was around today. Their passing was not a cause for sadness. However, a major act of sabotage in a large city in Kansas would have had a huge impact. Nevertheless, there was nothing I could do or say to encourage him to investigate this any further. I was not in his jurisdiction and he knew it. I thanked him for his time and asked him to keep me updated on any new developments. It was a courteous thing to say, although I knew it was useless.

All that was left for us was to keep doing our jobs as policemen and for me to make casual inquiries from Burke and Gordon when I encountered them, trying not to appear as though that was what I was doing. Being vigilant was always necessary in our line of work and even more so now. At some point we would hear something new, find a thread, think of a possibility, or maybe nothing at all would happen and the war would end and Eihan Hammerschmidt would wind up in Mexico, drinking tequila and learning to speak Spanish. For that matter, I might be there joining him.

A lot of our local guys were doing what they could in support of their country. Jess Meeker had been an accompanist with the Ted Shawn Men Dancers, toured all over the States, and even played at Carnegie Hall. He performed for the men at Fort Meade in Maryland while serving as an artilleryman. Jack Mitchell, who was all-state in football as a senior, dropped out of the University of Texas after only a semester to enroll in the army. Unfortunately, Pvt. Claude Bradshaw was killed in action back in September of '42. Then, we had just gotten word recently 1st Lt. Gilbert Hadley had perished as well, on the first of August. I knew Gil somewhat. He had been a friend of the Applebys and was a groomsman in Frank's wedding to Elizabeth Handy. He was so eager to join up and fight for his country. Kid was only twenty-three.

Two days after that news arrived, I got a surprise phone call. This time, Eliot Ness was reaching out to me.

Chapter Nine

When a true friend talks to you, there is a lighter tone in their voice, as though the friendship itself is not some kind of burden. However, I couldn't tell if Eliot had a highball or two before calling. This would be our first communication since I had sent him a congratulatory telegram. It was tough to determine his state of mind.

"Oh, Evaline is a doll," he responded to my query about married life. "She's teaching illustration to kids at the Corcoran College of Art and Design. And she still looks great on my arm. I mean, who wouldn't? What about you? Married? Prospects?"

"Still flying solo." I never thought about it until he mentioned it but a lack of a companion was more of a heartache than I realized. "What are you doing in D.C.? Law enforcement again?"

"Kind of law enforcement. Government job cracking down on prostitution. You wouldn't believe how many venereal disease cases we've got on some of the bases around here. It constitutes a whole new front." His sense of irony was in rare form.

"Is this a social call, Eliot?" I didn't mean to sound like I was rushing him, but I knew a conversation with him could wander from here to India and back again and not really accomplish much.

"In a manner of speaking." There was a long pause.

He knew I wasn't much for melodrama. "I could use a good man out here to help. You've got the brains and the drive for this kind of thing. Plus, well, I think we would get along famously. That is if you wouldn't mind me for a boss."

It was difficult to fathom how Eric Kimble, a tough Irish kid from the North Side of Chicago, entrusted by the ruthless leader Dion O'Banion, who took over the life of dear friend Baron Witherspoon and became a beat cop in a small town in Kansas, was now offered a job working alongside Eliot Ness in the U.S. government. The irony was thicker than an Oklahoma dust storm. It was a Ragged Dick rags-to-riches story as narrated by James Cagney or Humphrey Bogart. I doubt, however, Hollywood would be beating down my doors for this story. The dreams that had plagued me for so many years were a memory. All that remained were the scars on my face, a mask to hide who I had really been so long ago.

"It's an appealing thought," I responded rather honestly. In an instant, I read myself a fairy tale of giving up the drudgery of life as a beat cop, working to really have an impact on the war effort alongside an old friend and well respected man, and maybe just making something truly special of my life. I just couldn't see how the story ended or where it was supposed to go. That caused me to slam on the brakes.

"Of course it is. Can you imagine what we can accomplish? You could help me set up the third incarnation of the Untouchables. Might even get medals this time."

"Eliot, I've got a situation going on down here that desperately needs my attention now."

With genuine concern, he asked me for the details. I gave him as much of the story as possible about Hammerschmidt and our interview with his sister as well as the various "cohorts" and targets. His background and experiences would hopefully give me more insight than just four good old boys from a small town in Kansas and two tight-lipped federal agents. He admitted his current position didn't provide the same kind of clearance as he wished but was still willing to look into the situation on the government side as best he could with a few remaining trusted contacts.

"If you get this thing wrapped up, will you consider my proposition?"

"Of course."

I was a little dazed after talking with him, as though I had just gotten off a merry-go-round that was going as fast as a race car. It was everything: his exuberance, the possibility of working with him in Washington, the kind of advancement I would never get by staying in Arkansas City, maybe even the realistic chance for a social life. There was also Walter Reed General Hospital and Johns Hopkins, both of which were far better than anything within a hundred miles of where I was. Would it have been possible to get new surgery, maybe a new face, something that was neither Eric nor Baron? There were so many reasons to take Eliot up on his offer. I wasn't sure why I just didn't accept right there.

Then again, what would I do once the war was over? I couldn't see myself ultimately working for the government. What was I actually qualified to do? Maybe a job with the FBI? It seemed like I would wind up as a lost soul, floating around without any real purpose. I felt that way at times here, but at least I was liked and even admired, respected by my superiors and fellow policemen and the people in the community. Such a change of scenery wouldn't have done anything to set me on a path toward any kind of fulfillment. Besides that, who knew when Eliot would get divorced or move on to yet another city? Or perhaps I didn't have as much confidence in myself as I thought.

The thing that was worthwhile was finding any information that could be useful. I was unsure if I should mention him to Burke and Gordon or if it would look like I was going behind their backs. It shouldn't really appear that way, as we were all fighting the war together, or so it would seem. I wasn't even sure if I should talk about it with Chief Richardson and the guys on my team either. There was a faint hint of desperation. An enemy could easily smell that kind of fear.

I let Linda Kuchenberg, the police station's switchboard operator, know I might be getting another call from Mr. Ness, instructing her to inform me as quickly, but as quietly, as possible. She raised an eyebrow but seemed to enjoy the mysterious aspects of my comments. I smiled to take the edge off the mood.

It had been a long day, and I looked forward to taking off my shoes and catching an episode of *Nick Carter, Master Detective* on the radio. Always gave me a laugh listening to the fictional detectives. I was a block from the Elmo when I saw Agent Gordon walking toward me. He was more like ambling than anything, a relaxed gait I hadn't seen previously. I thought I also caught a small smile on his face.

"Alex." I nodded as he approached.

"Seems I recall you mentioned knowing where to find a decent drink in this town. I've tried but haven't come up with anything worthwhile."

I wasn't able to tell if that bit of a smile was from anything he had already tried. Then I wondered if all government agents were partial to a highball now and again. My only other experience with them had been Eliot Ness. I nodded my head in the direction opposite where we were, and we headed over to Junior's.

Just off the corner of Summit and Edgemont, with the First United Methodist Church in sight, we stood outside a nondescript building with only the numbers 1919 painted diagonally in red on the door frame. Agent Gordon looked around, saw the building next door with a considerably lower number, and turned toward me with a raised eyebrow.

"It was the year of the Volstead Act. Junior's opened up in rebellion. They still carry the same attitude all these years later."

"So close to the church?"

"Well, makes it easier for the pastor to duck in and out."

"What kind of place is this?" he asked bemusedly.

"The kind of place you were looking for."

Chapter Ten

Much had changed in the nearly twenty-five years of the existence of Junior's. It started as a place for men to drown their sorrows, the regular ones plus those that resulted from the fact they could no longer legally drink anymore. Men like me, coming back from the war with what they called shell shock, got lost in whatever concoction was at hand. A Fats Waller-type piano player or a small combo trying to sound like something out of Chicago for the transient gangsters that were hiding out gave it a lively atmosphere in the mid '20s and early '30s. It was a place where someone like Abram Dutcher, Der Kaiser, could mingle without being recognized, just another old vagrant in search of a drink. With repeal, it became another private club with no music other than the clinking of glasses and no B-girls trying to get you to buy them an expensive bottle of cheap champagne. The liquor, however, was top quality.

From the way he choked on the first sip of whiskey, Alex Gordon either hadn't had anything of quality for some time or I was misjudging the product. After clearing the tears from his eyes and the snot from his nose, he looked at me with the blankness of the dead and said, "Not bad." Maybe he knew more about hooch than I gave him credit for.

I got the bartender to pass us the bottle, and we

took a seat. It was not too far from where Jake Hickey held court with a band of fellow gangsters to plan various robberies in the region, much to the dismay of former Councilman Hallett and the late Kanotex president Martin Childers, the bogeymen behind the crime in Arkansas City. That is, not counting the Grandfather on the Hill, the mysterious and true source of all criminal power in the area, a figure I could not get even remotely close to. I stared at that table for just a little bit too long.

"Something wrong?" Gordon inquired.

"Just remembering the heyday of this place. Doesn't seem like all that much now, does it? Although the hooch is good." There were echoes of ghosts floating in the distance and faint outlines of ginks and girlies from a bygone era, just noises ringing in my ears.

"This is not your regular juke joint?"

I shook my head. Outside of Daisy Mae's and my apartment at the Elmo, I didn't have a regular place for, well, anything. Unless you count the police department in the municipal building, I guess I really didn't have much of a life.

"They used to call this town Little Chicago. More gangsters hiding out here per square mile than the 42nd and 43rd Wards."

"You know Chicago?" His look was blank but there was just a little something behind his eyes.

My reminiscing put me in an awkward position. Farm boys from Kansas aren't supposed to be familiar with neighborhoods in Chicago. Gordon had turned his lighthearted smile on, but his gaze continued probing just like the first time I met the federal agent.

"I had to learn a lot to tackle the likes of 'Crazy' Jake Hickey." It was a quick response to cover any uncertainty he might have had. I hoped it wasn't too quick.

"From the reports I read, he appears to have underestimated you." It was my turn to look perplexed. "We reviewed all the major officers of your department prior to making an appearance. It was important to determine the level of corruption before revealing ourselves."

"Now, wait a minute—"

"Suffice it to say," he interrupted, putting his hand up like a traffic cop, "the Arkansas City Police Department has had a spotless record since the late '20s. As far as we can tell."

Sadly, I wasn't initially concerned about the FBI's assessment of our officers as much as how in-depth their research had gone into our backgrounds, specifically mine. After years of struggling with a sense of identity and finally being at peace, his comments caused the hair on the back of my neck to stand at full attention. I focused completely on Hammerschmidt and the possibility of some kind of attack. Now I had to worry about closed doors opening wide open once again.

"Hickey was the toughest bird we've ever had to deal with." I wasn't sure where I was trying to get the conversation to go, so I poured us another drink. Being uncertain as to his capacity to hold his liquor like my friend, Eliot Ness, I may have been making a mistake.

"Charlie Floyd was all over these parts. So were Barrow and Parker."

"True. But they were all around us like a tornado

without ever really touching down. Hickey was living among us and didn't care a thing about anyone other than himself. After all, he was a true outsider." It was an ironic thought considering my own background.

There was silence for a moment as Alex looked around, taking in whatever bit of ambience remained. His head nodded as though in agreement with an unstated comment.

"You know, I want Hoover's job one of these days. I want to be the top dog and really show them up."

"Who?" It was a sharp turn in a different direction.

"All of those guys. You know what it's like being a Jew in the FBI? Oh, no one says anything directly to you, makes any comments about not seeing the horns on your head or being a Christ killer. That would be too obvious. The thing is they don't have to say anything. It's all the other little things."

"Like what?"

"Not selecting you for a weekend assignment because they think you're honoring the Sabbath, despite the fact you've told them you're available. So you wind up missing out on cases that could really put a feather in your cap and make you stand out. Then there are guys making comments about Eastern European immigrants from places like Russia, Romania, and Poland. All this talk about a propensity toward violence when all they are doing is perpetuating the myths of ritual murders like the Bellis trial. It's a different kind of blood libel, a kind of subtle prejudice to keep you in line but let you know this is as far as you go. We'll work with you, they're saying. But we won't let you be our boss." He slugged down his whiskey and poured himself another. "Yes, sir. I'm going to have Hoover's job one of these days." Junior's was still a place men could drown their sorrows even though the times had changed.

In some small way, I understood what he was going through. My ability to identify a killer in Ark City led to a request for my skills with the Wichita Police Department. My facial scars, however, caused those officers to automatically assume something negative about my character or training. While that was a limited situation, Alex Gordon had to live with being a Jew in a department that seemed to lack tolerance on an ongoing basis. His struggle was greater than mine, assuming I stayed in Ark City where people knew me, and didn't accept Eliot's officer of a position in Washington. It made me wonder all the more about my approval there.

At that moment, I understood Alex Gordon, what made him driven and what caused him to be reserved in his comments. He took in all that was said around him and analyzed it for his use. While Hollis Burke stood out front and center as the gregarious sort, Gordon was more than likely the real intellect between the two. It was a trait necessary to help prevent an act of sabotage. I just hoped he'd stop there and continue his climb up the federal ladder.

A couple of drinks later and I felt carefree, just the way I wanted to when I first encountered him in the street. I realized it was dangerous to get too relaxed around him, especially since I already considered him to be of higher intelligence and a generally suspicious nature.

"You ever get back to Chicago?" he blurted out, breaking the silence.

"I'm from Ark City." My response sounded like a dull thud.

"Oh, yeah. That's right. But didn't you have a kid in your squad from Chicago?"

"Yes. Yes, Eric Kimble. Heck of a soldier." The words felt like they were stuck in my throat.

"Surprising, given he was a heck of a gangster."

"I didn't get that impression." My response was just a bit too defensive of a guy who had supposedly died. Too much whiskey; too free and easy.

"Oh?"

"You know, we talked about our backgrounds, where we grew up. That kind of stuff. It was what you did to pass the time. I really sensed he was not all that interested in becoming the next Jake Hickey."

Gordon smiled and let out a small laugh.

"Kind of ironic that Jake Hickey, Kimble's boyhood friend, winds up hiding out in a town where that friend's sergeant is a beat cop."

"It's funny how the world turns that way." I heard my tone. It was dark and deep and no longer jovial. Gordon finished his drink in one swallow.

"Yeah. Funny. The world is definitely a funny place." Somehow, I didn't feel like laughing, and neither did he.

Chapter Eleven

Dave Morton and Evan Cobb had been scouring police records and incidents from various towns in the state of Kansas, anywhere north of us. That's the direction Hammerschmidt would be coming from. They came across a report of various tools stolen from a farm just south of Salina and non-perishable food items from a general store near McPherson reported by the owner, Jeff Carpenter. Then there was a medical bag taken from the back seat of a car owned by Dr. John Gardner in Hesston, and a run-down jalopy on the Mulvane property of itinerant handyman Michael Looper that supposedly hadn't run in nearly two years. These trivial thefts were in a direct line from Concordia to Ark City. Or Tulsa for that matter. Taken as a whole, however, they could be the accumulation of items for an escaped prisoner of war, even though we were uncertain how they all fit together. Unless he was doubling back north to Wichita, we had to assume he was coming here.

I had asked the two of them and Marcus Hayes to think beyond familiarity and beyond friendships to any and all possibilities for an accomplice. It was too easy to overlook someone simply because they might have been buddies or, at the very least, friendly. After my social outing with Alex Gordon and his sly innuendo, I didn't want to leave this in the hands of the federal agents. We decided to gather in a small meeting room at the police station.

"I wound up taking off the gloves for this one," Marcus started. "Most of it sounds petty to me. But, here goes. You've got Albert Guthrie. He's blond, like most Germans, and has a bad attitude. Again, like most Germans. Works as a machinist at Kanotex. That means he's got some skills. Charles Pearson. I think his cousin is the night man at the Elmo. He mumbles a lot and voted for Norman Thomas of the Socialist Party. Twice. I don't rightly know what he's been up to of late. There haven't been any reports filed on him or any complaints."

My smile was inward. I didn't want to disrespect Marcus' opinions or feedback. But hair color, attitude, and presidential politics were now the straws we were grabbing at. I made it clear to him this wasn't the right direction to go in. Fortunately, Evan Cobb's presentation was a little more thought out.

"Giuseppe Stevens is my top candidate. Moved to Arkansas City from somewhere back east in 1932. Records are sketchy and contradictory. Some say New Jersey while others indicate either upstate New York or the Bronx. He has had various jobs in machine shops and once worked for a construction company out of Winfield. His main job there was demolition with explosives. He is unmarried. Many factors point toward him."

"Yeah, but he's a drunk," Marcus interrupted. "He's one of those guys we look out for on Friday after payday. Can't hardly walk a straight line across the street. I can't rightly see him putting together a bomb."

Reminded me of my weekly run-ins with Rogelio Lopez back in the day. Despite having all the credentials, I knew Giuseppe Stevens, and he certainly was not responsible enough to be reliable for such a project.

"Okay, my second possibility is Miranda Vaughn."

"A woman?" Marcus Hayes' voice went up an octave. He was not what you would call a progressive thinker.

"Her late husband worked on several oil rigs in Texas and refineries in Oklahoma before they moved to Ark City in 1939. Now, assuming he was the actual contact, his sudden death two months ago of a heart attack might not have made it to Hammerschmidt. He would still be looking for Mr. Vaughn, so she would have to fill in."

"I'll buy that," I said. "But don't forget she is pushing sixty and hasn't done anything more dangerous than bake cherry pies and argue with her pastor regarding cussing as a sin." I looked toward Dave. He smiled.

"My list is a little longer." I nodded for him to continue. "Larry Bell and Jim Dorsey. We never could prove they were behind those rural bank robberies back ten years ago, but there were a lot of fingers pointing to them. That being said, if it was them, they're good with firearms and not afraid to mix it up."

Marcus rightfully pointed out German agents wouldn't have drawn attention to themselves in such a fashion. I had to agree. It was funny to think of Jake Hickey as a German agent.

"Tony Creamer, over at the packing plant. I found out his real name is Anton Kreutzer. Came over from Austria in 1927, first to Milwaukee for eleven years, then here in 1938. Now, he doesn't have a record of any kind, and I don't know what skills he has, but he fits the description of someone who might be an accomplice. He's mostly a loner. Not too many friends to speak of. Maybe Hammerschmidt would feel comfortable with someone like him." Dave turned a page in his notebook. "Daniel Field was a former employee of the Corporations Auxiliary Company. They were involved in industrial espionage and union busting. His employment card indicates his job title as Research Engineer. He came to Ark City in '33. That was the same year Mason Smith came from somewhere in California. Steady employee with no record of any kind. And I mean any kind. I can't find anything about him even in California. It's like, I don't know, he's invisible."

"You know, we know all these guys and Mrs. Vaughn. Until recently, we wouldn't have given them a tumble. Just all regular folks living their lives. Who would have thought someone who keeps to themselves would be considered a suspect?" This was frustrating me. It wasn't what we did, and yet the war and the things going on in this country made us sit up and pay attention. None of it could help the feeling of being lost.

"Maybe we're approaching this from the wrong angle." I was always willing to listen to the thoughts of Evan Cobb. "We thought, at first, as though Hammerschmidt may or may not be coming here specifically. Well, those minor infractions along the route seem to indicate he is targeting somewhere within our area. You figured correctly, Baron. There has to be an accomplice to guide him, someone who resides here. What we're doing now is pointing fingers at folks because of supposed flaws in their character or their prior work history. I think we need to refocus on targets. Why is Hammerschmidt coming here? What is he targeting and why?"

Even though I agreed with Evan, I was about to point out he had already made a list of potential targets we couldn't agree upon either. It was then Linda Kuchenberg informed me I had a phone call from Eliot Ness. It felt like the ice breaking over a lake at the first thaw in spring.

"You might have your hands full with this Hammerschmidt guy." Eliot was talking like an announcer for a college football game and expressing the abilities of a star running back. His enthusiasm for the skills and traits of an enemy soldier was alarming. "Worked in manufacturing back in Germany but was taking a degree in chemical engineering before that. Had to quit school because he couldn't afford it. Oh, and there has been a string of escapes from various POW camps involving Afrika Corps soldiers. Nothing has come of it. No incidents or sabotage. But it's awfully strange, huh?"

"What could they be up to?"

"Hard to tell. Something bad, naturally. I could speculate if it would do you any good. But I'm sure you've already got half a dozen ideas. Unfortunately, I'm not in the right circles to get much more information. What I'm giving you here cost me a night's worth of martinis with a Senator on the Foreign Relations Committee. Evaline was none too thrilled when I came home gassed. I told her it was all for national security."

"Did she believe it?"

"No. She never does."

"Well, you know I appreciate it, Eliot."

"And you think about that offer, Baron. It was legit."

I couldn't help but wonder how long his charmed life would stay that way. Then I wondered what we were going to do with Eihan Hammerschmidt when he got to town.

****

Lost in the Plains—Escape

John Schneiter had indicated to Private Stangel he needed his work detail especially early the following morning, perhaps an hour earlier at 6:30 a.m. or before if it were feasible. That didn't seem to raise any concerns with Stangel as he knew this was an important time of year for farmers. On top of that, based on the rotation, Private Friebus would be the supervising soldier. As things went, it was all a part of a soldier's life, and one soldier would be waking up far earlier than the other. Until the rotation came around to him again.

Schneiter brought out a set of clothing he prepared for his son Arthur as close to what Hammerschmidt had been wearing all along; Hammerschmidt approved. He also got a set of clothing his son would routinely wear when he went into town. Based on their approximate size, it would certainly fit the German.

The work detail arrived promptly at 6:30 a.m. Four of the POWs seemed unprepared for a day's work, still rather tired, with only a cup of coffee to motivate them; Hammerschmidt looked ready for an adventure, at the very least a full day's worth of work. The clothing he wore would match Arthur's clothing exactly, as had previously been discussed.

Mrs. Schneiter invited the men into the house for a

hearty breakfast she prepared. There were biscuits, scrambled eggs, bacon, orange juice, and plenty of hot coffee. Private Friebus took a small plate and hastily ate in a corner of the dining room, as he needed to maintain a proper watch on the crew. All the POWs ate rapidly as well since Schneiter had explained in German how busy the day was to have been and how they had a schedule to maintain. The latter comment only had meaning to Hammerschmidt.

"*Essen Sie gut. Wir haben viel zu tun. Es wird aber ein herzhaftes Mittagessen geben.*" (Eat well. There is much to do. But there will be a hearty lunch.)

As breakfast was finished, Schneiter quietly went over to Private Friebus and explained he would need to make use of Oberfeldwebel Hammerschmidt's skills to work on two tractors which had been performing poorly. Eihann watched all this and listened. As Schneiter was unable to afford to pay a mechanic and Hammerschmidt was qualified, it would be vital to the farm's interest to get these two tractors operational as quickly as possible. Regulations stated POWs on work detail were not to do any machine work. Schneiter again explained the farm would fail if the two tractors did not get repaired soon. Even after acquiescing on that front, the private was still uncertain about allowing one of his charges to be in the barn alone without supervision. Schneiter insisted, as the financial well-being of his farm, in fact his family, was dependant upon these repairs. His tone went from pleading to insistent to desperate. He swore he would take full responsibility and oversee the work. The soft spot in the private's heart melted enough to give in to the farmer's appeal. Schneiter was grateful, mostly for the fact he had no other argument to put forth in the event of a denial of his request. Hammerschmidt had grown quite impressed at the farmer's insistent efforts.

Shortly after 7:00 a.m., the work crew went outside to begin harvesting a new section of crop. "Hammerschmidt" went to the barn, tool kit in hand, head bowed under a large cap. Realizing he had promised the private he would continuously watch over the German, Schneiter instructed his wife to drive the '38 Dodge RC pickup and take the real Hammerschmidt as far as the county line as had been agreed upon. She begrudgingly agreed, never having previously embraced this plan as the correct thing to do.

Her driving was at best clunky, with difficulties shifting gears, jerking the two of them forward and back. It was not something she was used to. Neither was aiding and abetting an enemy soldier, even in the name of Christian charity. Hammerschmidt made no comment, smiled at her mildly to allay her concerns. The first part of the plan was finally under way. There was no further need of motivation or encouragement, just expediency.

As they got to the county line, he made a hand gesture encouraging her to continue in the hope he could reduce his distance to his destination. It was something he had planned all along, especially now with this softer woman in the vehicle. He felt he might be able to get her to consent.

"John said as far as the county line, mister. I can't go no further." Oberfeldwebel Eihann Hammerschmidt stepped out of the truck and tipped his hat politely. Inside, he burned with anger but thought better of retaliation. At some point, he expected his captors would discover his disappearance, and he needed the Schneiters to maintain their innocent ignorance of what had transpired. Mrs. Schneiter handed him a towel tied up at the corners. "Some bread and sausage," she said with a gracious smile, then forced the truck into gear, turned around, and headed for home, relieved the burden of this errand was over. Oberfeldwebel Eihann Hammerschmidt was out of the prison camp and on the road, but he was not yet a free man.

His anticipated pace, based on lighter weight than what would be carried on a loaded march, was not met completely. The county road heading north and south had more traffic than he anticipated. On those occasions of a passing vehicle, he slowed his gait to something more resembling an amble, kept his head down, and kept moving forward. A couple in a black Ford sedan, wearing their best Sunday clothes, offered him a ride. He debated accepting as he knew it would facilitate his travel. In considering the option, he preferred more of a truck or farm vehicle, as he could get along with the worker more than the churchgoer. He graciously declined, indicating he did not have far to travel. Their polite insistence became a bit of an annoyance, but his continued smile sent them on their way.

It was just north of Salina a farm truck did stop and inquire as to his well-being. The driver identified himself as Felipe Garcia, who worked on a farm nearby and was heading home for the evening. "Home" was a shack just outside of Bridgeport, a small unincorporated community less than twenty miles away. Hammerschmidt described himself as a migrant farm worker himself, forced to do so because of an injury that prevented him from war service and a wife who ran off. Those acting skills were paying off again. Garcia invited him to bed down, with a hot meal and an offer of speaking to the farmer he worked for.

Hammerschmidt accepted, as his food rations were running short and the only water he had was from streams he encountered along the way. However, he would have to avoid the job offer as it was back north, away from where he needed to be. He casually inquired as to how far it was from Wichita. When Garcia estimated it to be eighty miles, Hammerschmidt realized he had lost time and needed to make it up. He was grateful for the slop Garcia referred to as dinner as well as the opportunity to bed down unseen by anyone.

Farmers wake up early. Soldiers on a mission must wake up earlier. Given how far Garcia had to drive for work, Eihann woke up about 3:00 a.m., figuring he had about five hours of sleep, which was enough given the prior day was not too strenuous. He commandeered some bread and a thermos filled with water for this day, hoping to come across some kind of food elsewhere on this journey. Additionally, he took a few tools just lying outside of the ramshackle building. As far as materials to fulfill his mission, he was more than prepared. However, he desperately needed to get a lot closer to his destination.

A little more than an hour after his departure, he passed through the town of McPherson. Carpenter's General Store was off the road and away from residential buildings. At about 4:30 a.m., Mr. Carpenter was not ready to start business for the day. Hammerschmidt was able to pick the simple lock and find nonperishable goods along with a rucksack to make his appearance more reasonable. This food would sustain him for the remainder of his journey, assuming there were no additional diversions.

By the time he got to Hesston, it was just after 8:00 a.m. He stopped into a diner for a cup of coffee and piece of pie. The waitress was an older lady who seemed like she knew everyone in town. It was important to be seen as someone "normal" so as to be dismissed later. The man who hid was always viewed as a threat.

"Darned good pie, ma'am," he said in a perfect American accent. "Best I've had in a long time."

"Where you headed?" she asked as she refilled his coffee.

"Wichita. Got me a job lined up building planes. Should be able to get back on my feet before long. You know?"

"Good for you, son." She stepped away and greeted Dr. Gardner who had come in for breakfast before making house calls. Hammerschmidt's ears perked up at the customer's calling and noticed he didn't have his bag with him. Upon departing, he found the good doctor's car, windows all rolled down, with a medical bag in the back seat. A half mile down the main road, a colored man in a truck hauling hay to Newton offered him a lift. He now could put some distance between himself and the stolen medical bag and cut down the time lost along the way. If nothing else, a German soldier is punctual and knows how to keep good time. So much for the Italians and their railway system.

Hammerschmidt obligingly offered to help the colored man unload the hay. It was another way of presenting himself as "just another guy" who hopefully would not be remembered. While he spoke the language flawlessly and with an appropriate accent, the vagueness of this mission was such he needed to focus on viable options as much as reaching his destination.

Based on his forthright work ethic, the farmer the colored man worked for offered Hammerschmidt a late morning meal, and Eihann accepted. He had transferred the medical tools into the rucksack and tossed the bag into the farmer's well. After consuming a full meal, he was back on the road before noon. He looked at his watch and quickly calculated minutes and hours.

Late in the afternoon he made his way to the small town of Mulvane. He expected to reach it about an hour or two prior but determined it was necessary to bypass as much of Wichita as possible. Being a bigger city, there were too many possibilities of encountering policemen who were not as kind to strangers as the small-town officers might have been, or soldiers and airmen from the Air Force base nearby. The mission would have been over before it even got started.

Approaching 5:00 p.m., he passed a rundown house back off the road, a sign out front declaring MICHAEL LOOPER, JACK-OF-ALL-TRADES AND HANDYMAN. It seemed deserted, but he couldn't be sure. He had a notion of stopping and squatting for the night, but in the event the occupant still resided there he didn't want to cause a ruckus. What kept him fixed to the property was a jalopy in the back.

With some of the tools from the farm and others from Carpenter's General Store, Hammerschmidt quickly reviewed any difficulty with the engine. He brushed off the battery terminals and saw there was no corrosion. The tires were thin and without much tread, but solid. The wheels didn't have any give. The keys unfortunately were missing.

Hammerschmidt looked up from underneath the hood of the car, quickly glanced back out toward the street, and then walked around the property one more time, checking the doors and windows to the house. It was almost dusk, so his field of vision wasn't as great. He tossed his rucksack in the front seat and climbed in. He removed the ignition from the housing and detached it from the wire coupling. Using spare wires found inside the car, he hot-wired the starter and the engine turned over. By taking back roads, he could now become more invisible.

At this point, he calculated he was some forty miles from Arkansas City. Then he would have to find somewhere to hide. And wait.

Chapter Twelve

When you started seeing faces you'd looked at for twenty years as though they were strangers or aliens, something was definitely wrong. I couldn't be sure if it was the war, the intensity of having to deal with the FBI, or just me. The dreams came back again, images of mirrors cracked by my own reflection, mud-filled trenches, the late Baron Witherspoon forced forward by a shell exploding behind him and ultimately landing on me, barbed wire, and Jake Hickey and Heather Devore and Natalie Dixon. All this was more than likely due to stress. At least that's what Dr. Brenz said. When he tried to suggest I take some time off, he stopped me before I could respond. He knew how desperate a situation we were in and no one was going to be able to stand down. There was a war going on. For everybody. Even those of us with demons from the past.

The funny thing was I felt like a stranger, an alien, for so many years, after returning to Baron Witherspoon's father and becoming his son, knowing I was hiding and scared at the possibility of discovery at any moment, just waiting for the proverbial other shoe to drop. Certainly, I wasn't there to cause trouble, to undermine anyone's life. I was there to find a little moment or two until I could figure out what to do with my life, having already decided I was never really cut out to be a gangster. Now, all these years later, I was the one looking for the stranger. As the saying goes, it takes one to know one.

In the past, I would often visit with Chief Sims. He had been a City Marshal and Chief of Police back when Eric Kimble was stealing apples from vendors in the North Side of Chicago. It was Chief Taylor who would often reference George Sims as a mentor even to him. I took it upon myself to make my own introductions, being so bold as to knock on his door on South Second Street one afternoon in the early 1930s. He didn't seem to mind a total stranger on his doorstep considering it was a police officer seeking guidance. Even if I wasn't, it seemed the door would have been opened for me anyway. His trust and faith were unlike anyone I had ever known.

After suffering a stroke in November 1940, he passed away in early '41, well before the war had hit our front doorstep. His widow, Mrs. Mary Sims, didn't seem to mind my visiting now and then. She had already lost three of her nine children and kind of took me on as a sort of son, someone she got to look out for. It felt good to be part of a family, so to speak. She was an accepting sort of lady with a keen eye for the truth. Just how much of it she might have known never concerned me much.

There was no problem with my outlining to her the situation with the escaped German soldier. I'm sure Burke and Gordon would have been in a tizzy over "security clearance," but there was hardly anything in law enforcement she wasn't privy to through the Chief. She was the epitome of a police officer's wife. She was patient and understanding, could provide honest feedback, and knew how to keep silent on delicate issues. She also knew when to say the proper word or two to get you back on track. Having had to raise nine children on a police chief's salary was no easy task. From what I'd seen of her, she was just as tough as Chief Sims.

"Lots of bad men come to town looking for who knows what," she said. "You just got to plant your feet and stand firm. Remember when old Herman Barker got cornered in Wichita back in '27?"

It was amazing this seventy-seven-year-old woman was recollecting a thwarted robbery from sixteen years in the past. "Ma" Barker's oldest son, Herman, tried to rob an ice plant in Newton, got pulled over by a motorcycle officer in Wichita who he shot and killed, then wrecked his car. Rather than face prosecution, he killed himself. It was an example of law enforcement not giving in to violent men, whatever their intentions were. I knew that too well.

"And you," she continued, "facing down that bad character Hickey. George was real proud of you." The maternal look on her face indicated she was as well.

At first, all she was referencing were gangsters and criminals. It was what policemen dealt with. I was so caught up in believing Hammerschmidt was something different, more dangerous, and perhaps unintentionally buying into the "master race" notion. But he was nothing more than a criminal, an escaped prisoner that we would treat like anyone else in that position. The war and the idea that someone was in collusion with Hammerschmidt made it seem scarier. This reminder brought everything back into clarity. War or no war, what we as police officers were tasked with was to maintain law and order regardless of who was intent against us.

"How would Chief Sims have handled all this, ma'am?"

"I've told you the story countless times about the bank and the team of horses." She was referring to how Chief Sims brought stones to build the bank using his favorite team of horses. He did this while he was a police officer and when he was off duty. His dedication and persistence were the keys to getting the job done. She said everything without having to say anything.

I headed down to Daisy Mae's for lunch and saw the two FBI men who had just arrived. I asked if I could join them. After ordering, Burke spoke, sounding amiable but with just a touch of malevolence underneath.

"Now, we know you've been conducting your own investigation." I started to respond, but he held up his hand to cut me off. "Don't worry. We're not going to stop you. We're actually grateful for the efforts. Saves us a lot of time." I was getting a little perturbed at the notion they thought they had any ability to stop us from doing our job and wondered exactly what they had been doing this entire time. In the long run it wasn't worth it to ask.

"After this, you fellas get to go back home. This *is* our home."

"We get it, Baron," Gordon replied, trying to bring it all back to a bunch of guys sitting around having lunch. A quaint notion but one that just didn't set too well given how they already made their intentions known. "But don't forget, the United States of America is home to all of us." While Gordon spoke with an even tone, I resented the patriotic speech. The bottom line was the FBI wanted to catch the criminal, save the day, and take credit for everything, including all the legwork and investigating our local guys were doing. It was as though it were our duty to make them the heroes.

I finished my meal as quickly as I could, suddenly feeling as though the company was changing the way the food tasted. I made eye contact with Dixie who met me around back.

"Mind doing me a favor?" I asked.

"Sure."

"Any time those federal boys are in, try to get a handle on what they're talking about."

"You mean eavesdrop?"

"Sure."

"Well, I can get one of the…"

"No, Dixie. I need you."

"Me?"

"I'm getting to a point where I don't trust too many people."

She let out one of those laughs that come straight from the belly.

"Well, thank you for including me."

I smiled.

The city was big enough these guys might eat somewhere else. I don't know what came over me, but I had to know what they were up to. I just didn't want to be surprised if they made an arrest, whether it was foolish or not. Dave and Marcus and Evan and I had put in too much effort and thought we were coming up with blanks. Maybe we were on the right path and we didn't know it. Without this officially being a joint effort, I was starting to feel as though we were fighting a second war.

"Larry been in today?"

"Not yet."

"When he does, ask him to stop by the station to see me."

She nodded. I must have had the serious look on my face which she didn't see all that often. She realized things were starting to get dark and cloudy. That could only mean a storm was coming.

Chapter Thirteen

Chief Richardson allowed me to use his office to consult with Larry Hammer. He probably thought I was trying to determine if there was any relation to this Hammerschmidt soldier. What no one knew was his family background was English, with the poet Robert Browning as a distant relative. Larry wasn't too keen on anyone finding out about that tidbit. It might have ruined his reputation. Dave Morton saw him leaving as we were finishing up. He had a dejected look on his face.

"You don't think—?" I looked back as Larry walked through the station and then at Dave.

"No. Larry Hammer is just about the most patriotic guy I've ever known." I wasn't going to let on about his literary ancestry.

"So what then?"

"Well, several companies and plants have been using his skills for machine work. Repairs and maintenance. Shows you what kind of retirement he's been having. He gets around all over town, sees everything, and knows everybody. I mean everybody."

"So you're having him keep his eyes open?"

"Yeah. That and other things."

Dave pulled me back into Chief Richardson's office. He started to act like a father scolding his son for cheating on a test.

"Like what?"

"He hangs out at Daisy Mae's. The federal agents have been spending time there."

Dave shook his head, allowed himself to gape at the floor, before looking up and staring me in the face.

"They're not the enemy."

"They sure act like it."

"They are not the enemy," Dave repeated more forcefully.

Somewhere in the back of my mind, I realized I was bent out of shape with the FBI agents living in my town and claiming one of our residents was some kind of spy or traitor or saboteur, even though I realized it was probably true and had said as much. I could accept an escaped German prisoner of war coming to cause mayhem. Sure, that part made sense. The notion of a liaison being some sort of person living among us and waiting to do us harm bothered me. Instead of blaming a potential suspect, I was blaming the federal agents for bringing this scourge among us. I finally realized I had everything backward.

When you thought of it, Hitler was really to blame. He started a war and threw all the rules away. This wasn't like going after gangsters who were only interested in money. This certainly wasn't a man with a demented mind killing for a personal reason no one else could fathom. This was another country, intent on dominating the world and using whatever means they had. It was time for us to work together in order to protect Arkansas City.

"Okay, we're setting up a meeting with these guys. You get Marcus and Evan and have them bring all their notes. Better yet, see if Linda Kuchenberg can get them typed up. I want to look professional here. Everybody has got to lay their cards on the table. Everybody."

"What if they won't?"

"They will." I didn't know how I knew that, but I said it just the same. As usual, I was more hopeful than anything.

As Dave left, a patrolman advised me there was a call from a detective sergeant from Tulsa.

"Officer Witherspoon, this is Detective Sergeant John Clark from Tulsa. I've got a Suzanne Hamer here. Says she met with you before."

"Yes, we came down to question her about her brother. He's a German soldier who seems to have escaped from a POW camp here in Kansas."

"Yeah, well, she says she's got some letters from him that seem kind of, well, suspicious." We discussed those letters previously, so I was confused as to why they were important now. "She wants to talk to you."

"By all means, put her on."

"Here."

I couldn't be sure the information she had wasn't important, but going down and back to Tulsa would to take a whole day. We needed to keep our investigation continuing without any delays. I told Detective Sergeant Clark I would be down the next day and then advised Dave.

"So, it's either real information or a stall," Dave declared.

"One of the two. If it's the latter, that would assume she is involved somehow."

"Who said she isn't? I mean, we never checked her off our list completely, right?"

Since this thing began, all of us started looking at

people differently. Whether it was the people we had known for years or a sweet, innocent-appearing seamstress, it had gotten to a point where we were lost in our own imaginations. Watching too many movies at the Burford on a Saturday afternoon matinee had turned our thoughts from rational investigation to outright suspicion. This was one of the side effects of war.

I left at five in the morning. My heart beat fast, and I could feel my blood racing through my veins. It wasn't just the chill of the morning but the possibility of this excursion. I had to believe something would come out of it, otherwise it would be like spitting in the wind. For whatever reason, Suzanne Hamer was involved in this, whether intentionally or unknowingly. The only two constants were her and Ark City.

Detective Sergeant John Clark was a young man in his mid twenties, over six feet tall, very closely cropped hair as though he had been in the military, and had the look of American Indian blood in his family. His voice was the rich baritone I heard on the phone yesterday. His handshake was firm, almost aggressive. He tended to lean slightly forward.

"I have her in my office."

"Would you mind if I spoke to her alone?"

He gallantly waved his arm toward the office door. This time, Suzanne Hamer sat more demurely, not exhibiting the fire and confidence of our previous encounter, although Dave's absence might have had something to do with that. I waited for her to speak, considering she was the one who came forward.

"I found two other letters dated from very early this year. They seem to have been written around the time of some battle." She handed them to me and I started reading them while trying to pay attention to her. "It wasn't until after you left, and I discovered them, I decided to read them in light of what you had suggested. He mentions coming to see me."

"Perhaps he was just being nostalgic. If this was around the time of the Battle of Kasserine Pass, I'm sure he knew they were being overextended and either capture or surrender was imminent."

"But neither happened at that point."

When she said that, it was like a bell going off. In the other letter, he references Sidi Bou Zid whose battle was in early January. Though he describes confidence in the experienced soldiers in the Panzer divisions, he says "I hope I will get to see you soon." The earlier letter refers to an Allied retreat to Medjez on December 26, 1942. "Though it is a great Christmas present for our troops I would prefer to be spending that day with you. I am working toward that for next year."

There were conflicting comments: pride in the outcome of the battles and desire to be with his sister along with an indication he would, in fact, be seeing her. But even if he had a remote thought the tide would turn and capture was imminent, he would not have had any notion as to where a prisoner of war camp would have been located nor how close or far it might be from Tulsa, Oklahoma. It was more and more evident Hammerschmidt had been trained as a saboteur, had secondary plans when and if he were captured, and was laying the groundwork to throw off the authorities. Tulsa, Oklahoma, in the middle of the United States, would be a place the intelligence forces would focus on and thereby use valuable resources in apprehending him. The fact he wound up interred in Concordia strictly by chance and three hundred miles away from his sister gave the FBI the reasonable notion a target might be between the camp and her. It got all of us thinking that way. Was it dumb luck, or was he heading elsewhere?

"I need these." My tone sounded desperate. It was enough to give her leverage. "It throws a whole new light on this situation."

"I am coming with you." She did not state it as a request.

"Those," I said pointing to the letters, "are evidence in a federal investigation. You are not."

"You do not get them without me."

"At this point, you are not his sister. You are simply a diversion. If he needs a way out of a jam, he will use you. And then your life will be in danger."

"It already is. Can't you see that?"

I had no other option but to take her back to Ark City. She had known all along she would be going. She had a small valise packed, in Detective Sergeant Clark's office. It seems everyone had prepared for a journey except for me and my fellow officers. I consulted with Detective Clark before going.

"Have the seamstress shop she works at and her apartment watched. I really don't think she's involved with this, but I just can't be sure. I don't mind telling you, this stinks."

There was nothing he knew about her directly that would provide any reassurance as to whether or not I was driving back to Ark City with a conspirator. I had a seamstress with an escaped German POW for a brother and a few letters which were probably filled with lies. And about a hundred and twenty miles to think about it.

Chapter Fourteen

I learned silence does not yield anything fruitful. To sit in silence with an angry and confused woman would have been worse than questioning her and appearing to challenge her. She had one thing on her side, and that was bringing these letters to our attention. My thought was an accomplice would certainly not have done that. Unlike Dave, I wanted to believe she was an innocent dupe in all of this, that her brother Eihann was a German soldier through and through and would do anything or use anybody to accomplish a military mission, even an unwitting family member. Regrettably, in recent years, my trust in people did not yield too many rewards.

"Where do you think he's headed?"

"I haven't a clue. I don't know anything about war."

"I thought I did." From the corner of my eye, I could see her looking at me, perhaps wanting to inquire further. She was too smart to ask and reveal what she didn't know about life. "I was in the war in Europe back in '17. We fought the Germans then, too. Somehow it seemed different. I guess everything seemed different."

"How so?"

A smile crossed my lips. I thought of books from writers like Edgar Rice Burroughs or Robert Louis

Stevenson, tales of adventures where boys became men. They added romance to life and removed all of the horrors. After the war, I realized those were only tales.

"More heroic. More gallant. Like we were a bunch of knights defending something noble. I don't know. Maybe that's the way I wanted it to be. It was awfully hard to know what to expect when you had no idea what the world was like."

"That was over twenty-five years ago. Memory can play tricks on you."

She was more right than she could have imagined.

"Do you think he would listen to you?"

"About what?"

"If we had him cornered somewhere, would he listen to you if you told him to give up? Or, let's say we caught him, would he tell us who the other collaborators are?"

"It's hard to say. I can't tell if what he said in those letters had any heart behind them or if he is nothing more than a soldier doing his duty. You have to understand, Officer Witherspoon, I have been away for so long and do not have much of a relationship with him. He is a brother by blood only."

If that were the case, this would have been the most elaborate ruse an enemy had perpetrated. I began to think Germany planned for a war long before they ever initiated it, just as Abram Dutcher said. With smart and dedicated solders like Eihann Hammerschmidt, the ending might be farther away than we expected. We had been sleeping for too long, accepting the dreams of our way of life and abiding patriotism. It was time to wake up.

We passed the municipal building on the way to

the Osage Hotel. We needed to keep Suzanne safe yet accessible. She indicated she wanted to go to the station first and see what we had so far. It couldn't hurt us to have another set of eyes looking over everything we talked about and discussed endlessly. We wound up leaving her valise in the car.

Marcus, Evan, Dave, and Chief Richardson sat in the largest conference room we had. Agents Gordon and Burke joined them. The chief saw me and stepped outside.

"Is this Miss Hamer?" he asked.

"Yes, sir."

He turned toward her and tipped his cap.

"Very grateful for your cooperation, ma'am." His air of fatherly authority put her at ease, as though she were not in trouble for anything. He looked at the collected group and then back to me. "I'll attend to Miss Hamer in my office. I think you're needed in there." From his voice, he was basically telling me to walk naked into a lion's den. I decided to use an upbeat approach in the hope of generating some meaningful discussion and goodwill if that were at all possible.

"All right, gentlemen. Where do we stand?" I rubbed my hands as though I were ready to get to work, even though we had already been working intently with no results.

"Your officers have outlined the various and sundry background checks on civilians who might fit a particular profile." Burke, the heavyset jovial agent, now appeared uncomfortable in the role of professor. The eloquent words dropped from his tongue like cast-iron sinkers. I can imagine him really wanting to say, "You've given us a list of a bunch of no-goods and cronies."

"How does that match up against your list?"

"We don't have a list," Gordon responded in a very sober manner.

"We've had a difficult time interviewing several people despite the authority of our office." While Burke didn't sound right using elevated speech, this time his attitude was downright offensive. The arrogance he demonstrated was almost as bad as the Nazis themselves. Marcus Hayes didn't cotton to that much.

"Your office don't mean much to a bunch of hard-working folks who are just trying to make it through this war in one piece. Seems to me like you should be treating them like allies instead of possible criminals."

"They would do just fine if they cooperated." Gordon was practically at a whisper, the softness of his voice belying a disrespect for what he most assuredly thought were "little people."

"Who is the enemy here, guys?" I started to feel like the high school football coach giving his boys a pep talk at halftime when they were losing to their archrivals. "Look, we know these people. We live with them. We work with them. We can get them to cooperate. Why don't you just tell us what you need to know, and we'll help you get the answers?" Gordon and Burke looked at each other, their silence being a kind of unspoken language. "We're not in this for glory or for the spotlight. We're just trying to keep our community safe. That's all."

Burke leaned over, whispered into Gordon's ear. This was turning into some kind of sad comedy and hardly resembled an organized government investigation. After spending some time with agent

Gordon, I thought he might be more willing to allow us into their circle. When he didn't, I decided it was time to walk into it.

"Ever since you gentlemen arrived," I continued with a firmer tone, "you've done nothing to show us, as trained police officers, you have a handle on this. Seems more like what your agency did at Little Bohemia," I said, referencing the FBI's failed attempt to capture Dillinger, Nelson, and their gang at a rustic lodge in Wisconsin back in '34. "You haven't given us any indication you've got a plan of action. You told us you had sources and information but didn't say who or what they were. You use 'national security' as an excuse. Fine. We can accept that. To a point. You act like you don't care about the people of this town. Well, gentlemen, we do. This is our livelihood. Unless you're willing to include us in all of this, I think it might be better for you to just leave town, considering your investigation has gone nowhere. And, please, go ahead and try to convince me otherwise."

Burke reached into his inside jacket pocket, pulled out a folded piece of paper, and slid it forward on the table toward Dave.

"Those names," Gordon continued, "are likely suspects in terms of possible cooperation with the enemy. Their backgrounds, political leanings, and employment are all indications they could be involved. If you could offer feedback in the form of a report about each one, we might have a reasonable idea of where Hammerschmidt could turn when he gets in the area."

"If he gets to the area." Evan Cobb was still of the opinion Arkansas City was not the only location for an impressive act of sabotage. His efforts focused on reviewing all facilities within an accessible range. His attitude countered the shortsightedness of the Federal agents.

"For the time being, Evan, let's go on the premise Hammerschmidt is coming here. These agents have done their research and wouldn't just be here on a lark." I guess I was starting to sound like Cordell Hull. Maybe I'd have a future as a diplomat. Perhaps Eliot could connect me with the appropriate people. I fully intended on telling Evan to continue his efforts in case we overlooked something. We certainly didn't want any other community to be in jeopardy if we figured there might be a better target.

We adjourned the meeting with the indication of getting back together quickly to discuss our findings based on their suspect list. Gordon came up to me just as I was leaving, grabbing me slightly by the elbow.

"Who was the young woman?"

If I was keen on bringing this case to a resolution and was sincere about joint cooperation, now was not the time to hold back any information. There was Burke, who was blustery and friendly but in a sinister way. Gordon, on the other hand, was reserved but for a valid reason. Personality, I had learned many years ago, can be either a mask to hide the real person or the reason they were who they seemed to be.

I looked down at his hand on my elbow and then back up at him coldly. He dropped his arm.

"It's the sister of Eihann Hammerschmidt," I stated bluntly without elaborating.

Gordon seemed more impressed than surprised. Perhaps his attitudes toward small town police were changing.

"What does she know?"

"She has letters written by her brother prior to his capture. They seem to indicate he was going to come to her in Tulsa."

"Before he was captured?" I nodded. "How did he know he would wind up in a POW camp in Kansas?"

"Exactly what we were thinking. This thing is getting a bit trickier than we originally considered."

"Well, now we have more questions than answers. Did he allow himself to be captured as part of a spy ring for the purposes of terror attacks within the country? Or was it all just wishful thinking?" Gordon had an intense speculative look on his face.

"I don't buy the sappy notion of him wanting to give up being a brave German soldier and live in a small town with a seamstress sister. He was an ordnance man, very skilled. Don't you think he would have been better suited to his position in the Panzer Division?"

"One would think so. But Hitler's mind works differently than ours." Gordon's brows furrowed. He was in deep thought. "Are you familiar with Operation Pastorius?"

"No."

"June of '42. Eight Germans already living in the U.S. Two were American citizens. They all received intensive sabotage training through the German High Command. Able to use explosives, primers, and various forms of chemical or electrical delayed-timing devices. Pretty scary stuff when you consider it. They were given complex background histories and encouraged to speak in English at all times so they could fit in easily.

You know, be a part of their community. Their mission was to sabotage targets of economic importance. Hydroelectric plants, aluminum plants, cryolite plants, bridges, railroad stations, railroad repair shops, public facilities. You name it. It was a wide-ranging list."

"What happened?" This was all news to me.

"Two of the guys panicked and turned themselves in. They got off with long prison terms. The other six were executed."

"I had no idea."

"They had the training and the resources to put a lot of fear in people's hearts, Baron. Imagine what would have happened if those two hadn't ratted the rest out."

"Do you think this thing with Hammerschmidt is similar to that?"

"It's a possibility. The Germans must have numerous plans of this nature, and we can't stop them all. Apparently, the Afrika Corps is the key to this latest set of escapes. We have no idea what part Rommel might have in this, if any."

"But those guys didn't attack anything. They got caught."

"Correct. But it's like area bombing. They likely have countless numbers of these trained soldiers ready to go, make an attempt, fully knowing most of these are suicide missions. However, one of them might get through somewhere. Do you want that one guy to be Hammerschmidt and that one place to be here?"

I was an American, a veteran of the U.S. Army.

But I was also a law enforcement officer in the town of Arkansas City, Kansas sworn to protect the citizens of this community.

It wasn't my responsibility to stop all the threats to the United States.

Just this one.

Chapter Fifteen

I drove Miss Hamer over to the Osage Hotel and checked her in under an account we had through the police department. The hotel manager and front desk clerk knew not to interfere or offer any traditional services to anyone staying in that room but to call us if any calls came for them or any suspicious characters were loitering. On top of that, there would be a beat cop assigned to patrol the area regularly now that we had someone staying there. As I escorted her, I took a good look around and found it to be more nicely furnished than mine and wondered if I shouldn't upgrade. Then I realized I couldn't afford it on my meager salary.

"Anything you need?" I asked, sounding more like the bellman.

"No. Thank you. I've learned to live with less."

"By circumstance or by choice?" I didn't mean to pry. It was more of a casual off-handed comment, but the sadness in her eyes encouraged me to ask.

"First one. Then the other."

It was something I could easily understand. I started to leave, then turned back.

"I'm sorry to say this, Miss Hamer, but I don't think this is going to turn out well."

"Right now, he's nothing more than an escaped prisoner of war. If you capture him, you'll send him back. Probably in shackles." There was a slight smile on her face, possibly trying to believe what she had just said. I nodded as my way of accepting her fantasy. She called me back before I could shut the door.

"Have you ever lost anyone, Officer Witherspoon?"

I thought back to my Kansas farm boy buddy, Baron Witherspoon. There was Natalie Dixon and Jeannette Ross. Even, in some small way, Heather Devore. It was as though each person in your life props you up and keeps you going. When they're gone, you find another reason to move forward. I was still looking for mine.

"Yes, ma'am. Maybe more than my share, I suppose."

"I don't want to lose Eihann. We may have different beliefs, but we are blood. I can't help but think when this war is over we can somehow be a family again. At least I'd like to try."

"I hope for your sake that's true." I tipped my cap and left. I didn't want to think about loss any more. It would come when it would come.

My head felt clouded with a whole bunch of names, people who I knew intimately or vaguely, people who lived here in Arkansas City for at least five years, people who walked past you every single day who you wouldn't give a second thought about. Now I thought about them in so many different ways, imagining their words and actions as something less than innocent, a twist on what was meant to be normal, whatever that word meant anymore. Everyone had become the enemy. Now I was to become theirs.

I decided to take a drive around town and see if something would strike me as a possible target.

Refineries, the machine shop and foundry, the Keefe-LeStourgeon meatpacking plant, the Dr. Pepper plant, the Kist Bottling Company, even the Empire Steam Laundry. It was a pointless venture because I couldn't think like a saboteur. Then I castigated myself because I had worked out the vicious mutilation murders of three men back in '35 and helped Wichita police capture a multiple murderer in '38. I had the blessings of Eliot Ness himself as a qualified homicide investigator. Each time I could focus my mind on the case and see what the perpetrators saw, think like them and actually become them. I knew I had something, whether it was instincts or skill, but it just wasn't coming to me now.

In the end, this wasn't murder. This wasn't a single man—or woman, for that matter—with a deep-rooted hatred of something that we could pinpoint and track down. The ultimate goal of Eihann Hammerschmidt was to cause a disruption in the war effort while bringing fear to citizens of a small community who the enemy thought could not fight back or would not do so. I had to change my way of thinking so I could meet him where he would be. I had to understand him enough to think like him. But it had been so long since I was in a war; the stakes, too, had drastically changed.

I happened to drive by the municipal building and saw Dave Morton coming out.

"Hey," I called out to him. "Let's go for a drive."

He raised his eyebrows, shrugged his shoulders, and hopped in the car. We headed south on Summit and then turned west on Madison, passing by Daisy Mae's in the process.

"I thought you were springing for lunch." It was the first time Dave had acted casual, relaxed, and almost amused in quite some time. What we needed to do was directly check out locations that might be ideal targets. Our first stop was at Kanotex. I hadn't been to their offices since 1934. Back then, Martin Childers, the president of the company, had a large mahogany desk and a selection of the finest whisky even though it was still Prohibition. The current president had a smaller, more practical desk, no liquor anywhere in sight, neat and organized stacks of files in trays, and a picture of his devoted wife. There was scarcely any reminder of the late Mr. Childers.

We got a tour of the facilities and were impressed with the safety measures they had implemented. The management of the company was well aware of their importance to the war effort and took every precaution seriously. They had even created their own security force made up mostly of retired police officers from around the area who were only too happy to bring their skills to an important task. The same was true of the Keefe and LeStourgeon packing plant. Having considered those to be easier targets, Dave and I could breathe a small sigh of relief. There were still concerns, but they were mostly placated.

Our next stop was Strother Field Auxiliary #5, the South Field. The main field was located north of town, halfway between Arkansas City and Winfield, and was designated as a training base for both American and international pilots. This small airfield was just to the west of town, a largely nondescript area you could barely see from the main highway due to the access road being somewhat on an incline. There were French and Brazilian airmen in Daisy Mae's pretty regularly. They enjoyed the food once they were able to figure out how to order. Most of them spoke little English. All of them knew how to eat.

Running out of ideas for targets, I kind of figured something in the military was certainly a possibility. It made sense to me, considering such a target to be valuable to an enemy combatant. Dave, however, disagreed, figuring their security was far better than any factory, refinery, or warehouse. This drive was to be a test of that. Dave wasn't quite sure what I had up my sleeve. As we approached, a soldier stepped out from the shack at the entrance.

"Good afternoon, gentlemen." His greeting was welcoming, in my mind a little too welcoming. He was acting more like a maître d' at a swank joint in Kansas City.

"I'm Officer Baron Witherspoon and this is Officer Dave Morton. We're from the Arkansas City Police Department. We'd like to do a security check of the facilities, if you wouldn't mind."

"Not at all. Go right ahead, sir."

He waved us through, and we drove along an outer service road toward two buildings which seemed to be merely offices. There were larger hangars in the back of the airstrips, which were set up in a triangular pattern. Planes took off and landed intermittently while what appeared to be instructors on the ground talked with the pilots who had completed a flight. Other instructors used binoculars to observe airmen currently flying. Everyone in the facility was caught up in what they were doing. Outside of the guard at the gate, I couldn't tell if anyone even knew we were there. Dave and I looked at each other befuddled.

"Okay, so we got through," Dave admitted. "But

there's nothing but a bunch of planes here. And from the looks of it, largely trainers."

"We got through. Stop right there and think about it. This is just the auxiliary base, and we got through."

"We're police officers," Dave insisted.

"We've got uniforms and badges. The guard didn't check our credentials. You don't suppose security is this lax at the main field, do you?"

"Let's hope not."

We drove around a bit, getting as far as the hangars, before turning back and heading toward the main gate. We stepped out of the car and called out to the guard.

"Excuse me, Airman…"

"Cooper. Brian Cooper, sir."

"Yes, well, Airman Cooper, we're a little concerned about security around here."

"Oh? How so, sir?"

"Yeah, we just waltzed right through, pal." Dave should not have sounded so glib. I guess the whole situation with Hammerschmidt got him that way. "Danced our way in like Fred Astaire."

"Not quite, sir." Dave and I looked at each other perplexed and then back to Airman Cooper. "I have two buzzers in the shack. One goes directly to a Chief Richardson of your department. The other goes to my security team." He turned and waved somewhere in the direction of the two office buildings.

"I'm sorry, Airman Cooper," I said politely, "we didn't see any security detail."

"No, sir, you wouldn't." He made a gesture with his arms, some kind of signal I suppose, because the next thing that happened was a shot landed at my feet and then at Dave's. "Senior Airman Mayer and Technical Sergeant Donnelly are the two best marksmen I have ever seen. And believe me, sir, I have seen a lot."

Both Dave and I froze in our respective spots. We had grossly underestimated the security at this small airfield.

"Thank you for the demonstration, Airman Cooper." I was gracious but eager to get the heck out of there as soon as possible.

"My pleasure, sir." He had a satisfied smile on his face as we managed to find our legs and willed them to move. Dave and I didn't say a word on the way back to town. Upon our return to the station, Chief Richardson had a smile so similar to the young airman's it made me think there was some relation to Airman Cooper.

"So what now?" the chief asked.

"I'm just not sure anymore. We've tried to scrutinize people. We've tried to figure out places. Those federal agents aren't giving us anything other than a bone to chew on. This kind of investigation is out of our league."

Apparently, my response was not acceptable to a man who had been my boss for the better part of nine years. Lester Richardson was tall, stout, and strong. Not just physically but of will as well.

"Again, I ask you, Officer Witherspoon: What now?"

He was not going to let us give up and just sit and wait. If we did, it would be too late by the time something actually happened.

Chapter Sixteen

It was something new, not to me personally, but to the small team the chief had me put together. I called the guys for a meeting in the conference room. Marcus was already there, eager to do something, anything rather than all the talking. His fingers strummed on the table, not as much out of boredom as eagerness. He was not the kind of guy to wile away the time casually. Dave and I walked in at about the same time, a similar look on our faces as though we had just gotten off a Ferris wheel. Evan came in last, hauling in a pile of folders.

"What are those?" I asked.

"These are the most viable suspects who…"

"No." I didn't mean to sound so abrupt by cutting him off. "We're doing something different." Evan dropped the folders down on the corner of the table, half shrugged, and sat down. It didn't seem to matter much he'd put in a lot of hours of research and ignored his wife and kids for a day or so. "When did you start here, Evan?"

"October of '36. Right before Arkalalah."

"So you weren't a cop in '35 when we had those grisly murders."

"No, I wasn't. But I remember reading about them." He seemed to shiver as though a North wind had blown through the room.

"That wasn't pretty," Dave chimed in. "Not from the first to the last."

Marcus was growing impatient. "Well, I was here. So what? What do a bunch of violent murders from eight years ago have to do with this situation?"

I sat at the head of the table, gathering my thoughts, my fingertips touching each other as though I were trying to get us all to focus on something different. Either that or a psychic at a séance.

"I sat and looked over all those reports and tried to imagine what kind of a person would do that. Tried to get inside their head."

"I've read the reports, Baron, and your work on that case was astounding. But I've got to agree with Marcus," Evan responded. "This isn't a murderer we're looking for."

"No. But he has a motive. He has a cause. He has a purpose. And we've got to figure out what that is." I had Eihann Hammerschmidt's file with me and slid it across the table to Marcus. "Read about this guy. His background, his education, his military service. Put yourself in his shoes. How would he escape? What would he do once he was out of the camp? Where would he go? Is he actually coming here? If so, what are his plans, his objective? Is there an escape plan or is this just a suicide mission?"

"You expect me to figure that all out by reading his file?" Marcus sounded incredulous, on the edge of outright telling me I was crazy. He had been a police officer for a long time. All he knew was walking a beat and arresting law breakers. The new kind of criminal investigation, advocated by none other than Mr. Hoover, involved an analytical thought process. I hoped

Marcus would get onboard with the notion.

"Yes. Look, you were military just like me. You understand how that kind of mind works. Use that experience. You might understand something about this guy."

"Great. I get stuck thinking like a Nazi."

"But that's just it, Marcus," I came back. "Maybe he's not even a Nazi, just a soldier. Your report from the camp indicated a lot of those prisoners are just kids drafted into the army. I'm pretty sure most of them have no idea what Hitler actually has in mind." Marcus nodded in acceptance and opened the file.

"What do I get?" Evan asked. There was a slight smile on his face in anticipation of a tougher task. I hoped he wasn't looking forward to more time away from his wife and kids.

"Rather than go through all those files," I said, waving my hand over the pile he brought in, "create an image of the type of person who would help. Like you're writing a comic strip in the Sunday papers and you need to create a character. There is a particular kind of person who would be involved with this, both mentally and intellectually. Someone with a mindset of turning against their country as well as having the resources to assist Hammerschmidt."

"So you don't want me to look through the files and figure it out that way?"

"We've all got these ideas in our heads on people that have been discussed over and over again. This is like making an outline and filling in the blanks. You figure out what kind of person we're looking for, and then we'll find the person."

I wasn't sure how well the guys took this. I glanced

over at Dave, who knew what we had gone through eight years ago, how we read Dr. Brenz's reports repeatedly and talked and speculated and made guesses. We didn't start by reviewing criminal records and then trying to fit a suspect into the case. This wasn't the type of investigation Marcus had any experience with but, head buried in Hammerschmidt's file, he at least showed a willingness to try. Evan took a note pad and started writing feverishly, the ideas pouring forth. There was no way to tell what this would lead to, but we needed to do something different.

Dave and I went in to talk this over with Chief Richardson, who also had a military background. I asked him what he would be doing if he were a German soldier wandering around practically lost in Kansas. I didn't know why I hadn't reached out to him earlier.

"Whatever else he may have done, he certainly didn't walk off Schneiter's farm in his prison garb. Right now he's got on worker's clothing."

"He'll blend in that way," I said, nearly choking on my own words.

"Exactly. He wants to be just another Joe, a poor itinerant worker, a bum, someone you might not even notice or, if you did, you wouldn't remember much. A guy you might even feel sorry for. And because of that, he's probably right out in the open, hitching rides, but at the same time keeping a low profile."

"At some point he's going to need..." Dave's thought was starting to drop off. "Tools. Right? I mean, whatever he's got planned, he'll need, I don't know, what do saboteurs use?" Our ignorance on the mechanisms of modern warfare was evident.

"He could use all manner of devices," the chief

went on, "from fuses to wires to an alarm clock hooked up to sticks of dynamite. He was an ordnance man, right?" I nodded affirmatively. "That doesn't just entail handling large munitions but machines as well. He's a skilled craftsman, hence the alarm clock example. Now, that alone might not do major damage. But if it triggered bigger explosions…"

"Like at a refinery?" I suggested.

We kept talking like this for an hour or so, almost as though we were playing some kind of a children's game. A shiver ran down my spine at one point, recalling the case of the brutally murdered men. The image I had created in my mind was so far removed from the sweet and demure Natalie Dixon. Perhaps I could have reasoned it out earlier but my (dare I say it?) love for her clouded my judgment. There was nothing like that now. The frustrations of this situation egged me on, daring Hammerschmidt to come into my jurisdiction so I could capture him and stop his plan.

Dave wrote down what we said, as we were going too fast and someone needed to keep track of these ideas. As planned, our team met later in the day to see where we were at. Dave read off his notes first.

"I agree with the chief for the most part," Marcus replied. "But this guy's ability to speak English is scary. Especially if he does it without an accent. He could fit in anywhere. Personally, I'm surprised he didn't head out to Victoria."

"Why's that?" Dave asked.

"Well, first of all it is a largely German community. If he presented himself as from a German background, you know, far background, not from Germany directly, he'd be taken in. I've got no doubt those folks feel a little heat on account of their heritage, whether they agree or disagree with that Nazi paperhanger. They're probably wondering if they're all going to get locked up, like the government did with the Japanese."

"The Japanese can't hide their heritage. The Germans can." Evan had a point.

"Well, beyond that, there's Walker Army Airfield out there. They train for the B-29s there. I'm sure they're going to get around to using those big boys on something important pretty soon."

I looked at Dave and then Evan. I can't say it was fortunate he seemed to be moving in our direction, but disruption of bomber flight training could be more advantageous to the Germans. So then why was Hammerschmidt heading here? I looked over at Evan, who was ready with his recital.

"You know, my first thought was any accomplice had to keep a low profile. I mean, if you're hiding in the shadows, you don't want to be forced out, right? But then, if you figure Hammerschmidt can't keep popping his head up like a prairie dog everywhere, the accomplice can't be so low profile as to not stand out, either. We still haven't determined if a collaborator has been pre-arranged and already known to Hammerschmidt. No, I figure whoever might be helping him has to be, well, a regular guy. Or gal."

"How do you mean?" I wasn't sure where he was going with this.

"You know, someone you might encounter every day. No one like Hallett. He's different. After reading your old reports on him, I pegged him more as the corrupt gangster type. He seemed to be into corruption for monetary gain. I don't think betraying your country pays as well." Though not trying to be comical, Evan couldn't have been more correct. "I'm thinking someone more like Larry Hammer…"

"No." I didn't mean to sound short with Evan, but I wasn't going to even allow this kind of speculation. "I've known Larry Hammer for going on twenty years. There is nothing about him that smells the least bit dirty."

"Well, I mean, he is involved with just about every…"

"It's not him, Evan. I'll swear on a stack of Bibles to it. He was born and raised here. Doesn't have a thing to do with anything German. Other than drinking beer." I could sense Dave looking at me, wondering why I sounded almost angry. Made no sense for me to go off like that, especially if there was just the slightest possibility I could be wrong. "What else have you got?"

"Okay," Evan continued, apparently trying to prevent himself from getting upset with me in return. "I think whoever this accomplice may be is someone who we encounter regularly. Because if you see that person in the street or driving toward Kanotex or going to a hardware store, you're not going to think they're doing anything suspicious. They've got to be able to access and go where Hammerschmidt needs them to go without drawing attention to themselves."

There was a dazed pause in the room. It felt like we just took our final test for the semester, and we were all going to flunk.

"Anything else?" My question was more of a gasp than an inquiry.

"I'd say he has a truck or large vehicle. We can't

be too sure what the target might be and what kind of equipment he'll use. Let's assume it's going to take something more than a Zippo."

"Just about everyone in town owns a truck, Evan."

"Yeah," he responded, his voice dropping off like falling down a well.

"So the majority of people we were looking at are probably not in the mix?"

"Exactly."

"Basically, we're looking for a nice guy—"

"Or gal."

"—who wouldn't hurt a fly but who might be helping an escaped German POW blow something up in Ark City." I looked around and saw three perplexed faces who finally realized we were looking for a needle in a haystack.

Chapter Seventeen

I was in the conference room by myself, looking over the files I had told Evan to forget about. There was something to what he said but also a feeling gnawing at me I somehow had crossed paths with this unknown accomplice. Over the years, in my effort to be "just one of the guys," I made it my business to be as much a part of the community as I could bear, the discomfort of my facial scarring notwithstanding. I knew a lot of people, and they knew me.

A very determined Agent Gordon walked in long strides directly toward me. He opened the door brusquely. I attempted to make intelligent conversation, but he had other plans.

"We've come up with some ideas—"

"Never mind that. We're going for a drive." It seemed more like an order than an offer.

We drove north toward Winfield. I wondered if we were heading toward the Cowley County Courthouse for some records or to meet with a prisoner in the jail who might have some information. Whatever it was, I wasn't privy to it since he didn't utter a single word. His demeanor was serious yet reserved. As we approached Strother Army Airfield, I got the impression he was going to let me in on something. We parked just outside the gate.

"Officer Morton and I already went to the auxiliary

airfield. They've got good security. We found that out the hard way." Someone had to break the spell of this obsession, so I figured it would be me.

"The auxiliary field has one building, a couple of hangars, and a bunch of untrained Brazilian pilots. This place has four Quartermaster buildings and two instructional buildings with a student capacity of over five hundred. There are day rooms, an officers' club, a theater, a chapel, a bowling alley, and a gym. Housing can accommodate over four thousand men. Not to mention a gasoline storage capacity of over two hundred thousand gallons. It would make for one heck of an explosion, wouldn't you say so? This is a small city as well as being a military base. This, Officer Witherspoon, is the target."

"And you know this how?"

"We have sources."

I felt my eyes narrow and my jaw drop open. It was a combination of anger, disgust, and frustration I'm certain appeared on my face. Were we, the officers of the Arkansas City police department, merely pawns in this game the FBI was playing? Why did Gordon even bring me here?

"This is ridiculous, Gordon. You walk into my police station telling us about an escaped German POW and basically insinuate we should stay out of your way, that it was just a courtesy call. But you're unable to do anything because the citizens don't trust you. Well, imagine that. Then after agreeing to let us help, you take none of our suggestions even though countless man hours went into providing a detailed analysis based on our intimate knowledge of the city and the area. And now some unknown source, which you have never identified, points you in the most obvious direction possible, a place that has a great deal of protection built into it by the military itself. You can't do this to us, Alex. This is not some game to put feathers in your cap, show them how successful a Jew can be."

"This has absolutely nothing to do with that. Look, Witherspoon, I'm telling you this as a gesture of good faith. The truth is we don't trust anyone. We can't afford to." They were only words but felt like a cold slap in the face. At this point it was getting hard to take the threat of an escaped German POW seriously. "You, for example. You were in the war and served with an Eric Kimble, right?" I nodded. "He had connections with the Market Street Gang which eventually turned into the North Side Gang. Did he tell you any of this?"

"Come on. That was twenty-five years ago."

"Did he tell you any of this?"

"What are you driving at?"

"Only this: there's no record of Eric Kimble after the war. No discharge papers. No death certificate. No document indicating he was AWOL. Nothing. It was as though he just vanished from the forests of France."

"Again, Agent Gordon, what's your point?" I remained steadfast and defiant, but I could hear my own heart beating and wondered if he could as well.

"Let's suppose for a moment you wanted to help a buddy out. Hey, it's war and you're all suffering through the same trials and tribulations. You become like brothers. A guy says he got in with some bad fellas back home and wants out. Joined the army looking for an escape. Figured he might get killed and die honorably. That would be heroic, right? But maybe, just maybe, he might live. What then? So this other guy, this real nice Kansas farm boy tells him not to worry and he'll help sneak him out so he can live his life somewhere in peace, not be bothered or troubled by his past. What was the harm? It was only helping out a buddy, right?"

"Some fairy tale there, friend."

"The point is, friend, you had a connection with a Chicago gangster who seems to have disappeared from the face of the earth. Twenty-five years or no, you stand out as someone to watch. Do you see where I'm coming from?"

"Then why bring me here?" I said, feeling the sneer on my face.

"Because sometimes I'm wrong." Without a bat of his eyes, he stepped out of the car and walked toward the front gate, flashing his government credentials like they were the Holy Grail. "Lieutenant Frank Donaldson is expecting me," I overheard him say as I approached from behind. The guard at the booth made a call to somewhere inside the base. As Gordon turned to look at me, there was a dismissive smile that didn't quite settle in with my seething anger.

"This is the way we think, Witherspoon. This is the way we are trained to think. Do I believe the fairy tale? It's pretty fascinating to consider. But, no, I don't believe it. However, if we don't look under every rock, the Germans win this war. If your feathers get ruffled in the process, that's just too darn bad. You've got to look at the much bigger picture. Our freedoms and our way of life are at risk here. You get it?"

Right then, I understood him. He had already told me how difficult it was being a Jew in the FBI, the way other agents treated him or thought lesser of him. He had accused me of something that was almost close to the truth. At this point in my life, it wouldn't have mattered if my background as Eric Kimble came to light. What I didn't want to be accused of was being a German collaborator.

Second Lieutenant Donaldson was a good six foot four with shiny black hair and pronounced jaw and cheek bones. He could have easily been the next star out of Hollywood if he weren't one of the premier trainers. I'm pretty certain the Army used his image in recruitment posters.

"Major Vance wanted me to extend you every courtesy, Special Agent Gordon, but wishes to reiterate we are an extremely secure base." The guy also had a great voice. Probably was a crooner in the Strother AAF Band. "We have multiple layers of security and round-the-clock guard posts. We feel quite comfortable."

"I am absolutely certain you are, Lieutenant Donaldson," Gordon responded, equal to the smoothness and charm. "However, we need to remain on high alert until this prisoner is apprehended. There's too much danger to be dismissive in our need to be vigilant."

"What if for some reason he isn't captured?" While it was a valid question, Donaldson's insinuation had an underlying tone of annoyance. "It's a big country. And you had referenced a relative in Oklahoma, correct?"

"He will be captured. I assure you." Gordon stood his ground, looking directly at Donaldson for what seemed like an inning of baseball. The FBI man turned toward me by way of introduction. "This is Officer Witherspoon from the Arkansas City police department.

He is our liaison while we are here."

Finally having a legitimate title, I walked by Gordon, reaching out to shake the lieutenant's hand.

"What do you think, Officer Witherspoon? Can an escaped German prisoner of war infiltrate a heavily guarded military base?" My newly created position of liaison now placed me between two government employees, so to speak, in an effort to give bragging rights to one. I was about ready to resign my new position.

"Agent Gordon has trusted sources which I am neither willing to dispute nor discuss in detail." I got a sly smile from Gordon out of the corner of my eye. "Just the same, I don't think it's completely safe to disregard other targets in the area. You see, it all depends on the ultimate ends."

"How do you mean?" Donaldson pressed. I felt like I was on stage at the Burford and the spotlight was on me. Finally, someone was willing to listen.

"If the efforts of these saboteurs are to impact the war effort, your facility is a likely target, probably the most likely in this area. I'm certain you would agree. And despite your confidence, there are perhaps ways of accessing key buildings." He started to defend his castle, but I continued. "On the other hand, if fear and terror are the keys, getting the general citizenry afraid, as it were, factories and refineries would make an impressive explosion, don't you think?" I smiled as though I had just told a punch line to an unfunny joke.

While trying to figure out if I was serious or crazy, his eyebrows furrowed.

"What did you mean by 'these saboteurs'?"

Gordon pushed forward again.

"May we see Major Vance now?" With that, he led us onto the base and toward the main headquarters. Lieutenant Donaldson casually looked in my direction periodically, wondering if he should pursue the comment further. It was apparent the military command at Strother had not been advised of other escaped German POWs. For the life of me, I couldn't figure out why.

This whole thing was looking more and more like some kind of twisted game. After the war was over, they would dismantle the base, the FBI would head back to the marbled halls of Washington, and the people of Ark City would be left behind to clean up the mess. It wasn't a game I grew fond of playing but knew I needed to see it through to the end.

Chapter Eighteen

There was a mixture of apprehension, fear, and relief. The kind of uncertainty that comes when something long hidden, never discussed, and barely remembered comes to the front of your mind, superseding all other thoughts, desires, plans. Did Gordon actually know something or did his research just point in a general direction? And was he pointing at me? Did the fantasy he wove make some sense to him? Maybe he simply decided to use it to stir the pot, get a reaction, and perhaps uncover something he wasn't even looking for. There was nothing to worry about as far as revealing the so-called truth. I was never a full-fledged member of the North Side Gang in spite of my close friendship with Dion O'Banion. Sure, a sneak thief with the Market Street Gang, but a good son who never stayed out late. Not too late anyway. On top of all that, I volunteered for the army, went to fight the Hun in France. Would the people of Arkansas City think anything less of me, even after I had taken over the name and identity of a favorite son of the city?

I wasn't going to wait to find out. Whatever else was going on, I knew I would not be happy accepting my fate if the truth actually came out. As much as I had done as a police officer and as good as I had been to all the members of the community, my natural thoughts were of committing something akin to an unpardonable crime. It was important for me to find out what these FBI agents knew and decide from there what the most important thing was between the war effort and my life.

My first thought was to reach out to Eliot Ness, try to determine if there were any open investigations into gangsters from back in the day. Then I realized he was so far removed from criminal investigations of that sort I would be wasting his time and mine. Sandy Clevenger had a wealth of resources available to her, but I doubted her reach extended deeply inside the sanctified halls of the Justice Department. It was best to face this thing head on, like a bull in a china shop.

My stride up the stairs of the hotel sounded like troops marching. My dander was up, and my attitude was one of defiance, even though there might not be anything to be defiant about. I knocked loudly.

Agent Burke opened the door with a perplexed and somewhat annoyed look on his face. He stood there, without a verbal greeting, waiting for me to break the ice or state my case. He had the patience of a saint.

"I'm looking for Agent Gordon."

"He's out, Witherspoon."

"Where?" Burke shook his head. His lack of response and his ambivalent attitude started to make me hot under the collar. "Don't you two work together? Aren't you some kind of a team?"

"We tend to follow our own leads. That is, if it's all the same to you."

With Gordon not around, I needed to come up with an excuse for being there and barging in like I did. I would take the matter up with Gordon when I saw him. I related the visit to Strother AAF base and Gordon's concerns over security as well as the encounter Dave

Morton and I had at the auxiliary base.

"I just don't see how one German soldier, even with an accomplice, can gain access and do any damage. Even lobbing grenades over the fence, he's not going to make a big enough impact to warrant an escape and traveling all that distance."

"Yes. I see your point." Burke sat down on the edge of the bed, still holding on to a file he had been reading when I knocked. "This is where Agent Gordon and I, shall we say, don't necessarily see eye to eye. A small commando force coming to a city on one of the coasts and making such an effort, yes, that I can see. Assuming such a force existed. But these random escapes appear to be more designed to create terror and fear in communities and cause valuable resources to be expended." It was the most accessible Burke had been since he arrived in town. "Until now, the escapees haven't even been afforded an opportunity to commit any acts at all. Perhaps they didn't have the resources or maybe they just lost their nerve. As there are targets far easier to access, I feel we can safely eliminate the base."

"Of all the places around here, I've been focusing on Kanotex."

"The refinery?"

"Yes."

"Yes. Very good call. Makes a certain deal of sense. An explosion there may not impact the war effort too greatly, but it would be a hell of a show." I couldn't tell if he tried to be funny or ironic. Nevertheless, in spite of the fact I felt as though this were the right direction, I opted not to go into too much detail, figuring to go back to the guys and focus our efforts where we felt it was worthwhile. As I started to leave, Burke asked me if I had a message for Gordon.

"No. That's all right. I'll find him later."

My first thought was to head back to the station, but then I decided it would be better to talk to Larry Hammer and see if he could give me some insight as to what it might take to blow up Kanotex, as strange as that sounded. He knew the ins and outs of that place plus half a dozen other factories and warehouses. His knowledge of machines could guide me toward a better direction, considering now I knew Burke's feelings were the same as mine.

Larry wasn't spending as much time at Daisy Mae's as he had been in the past, on account of his being on call all over the place due to his various skills and abilities. Nevertheless, it was still the best place to start.

Dixie actually had to wait on tables, considering she had a diner packed with workers and air force pilots from all over. I heard a group of French guys and something that was probably Brazilian, not being sure because I didn't know what Brazilians sounded like. It almost seemed like each group was trying to outdo the other with their noise and gestures. I remembered the French girls more than the French soldiers from my war days. They weren't nearly as loud. I took the only seat left at the counter. Ralph Houseman brought me a glass of water and a cup of coffee.

"You eating today, Baron?" He seemed almost breathless from the constant business.

"Looking for Larry."

"Ain't seem him in, like, two days. Best as I can remember."

I figured this was as good a spot to hang out as any, considering there were many people floating in and out all day. After close to an hour and four cups of coffee, it started quieting down. Ralph looked like he had been at a track meet. For a kid who showed up five years prior just looking for a job, he certainly had his hands full. He didn't appear worse for the wear. I guess the younger guys were in better shape for this sort of thing.

"You sure you don't want something to eat?" I shook my head. "You know, Larry might not be around for a while."

"I figured. Hey, let me ask you something."

"Sure."

"Lot more people in town now, right?"

"Well, yeah. Workers, pilots, the whole lot."

"Anyone that doesn't…you know, look right?"

"How do you mean?" An honest kid like him wasn't as jaded as the old guy I was turning into. He probably couldn't wrap his head around the notion a hard-working man like himself would be here in town to blow something up and cause a melee.

Nevertheless, his question was valid. Even trained law enforcement officers hadn't been able to put together any kind of clear picture of who we were looking for, outside of the escaped German prisoner. How could I answer?

"If a German or, let's say, an Italian prisoner of war came here, would you recognize him?"

"Sure. They talk funny."

"Okay, fair enough. But what if the guy spoke English real well? Maybe didn't have an accent. Would you still be able to tell?"

"I don't know what you're getting at, Baron. Either

a guy's a foreigner or he's not."

"There's all kinds of foreigners, Ralph." I had a fifth cup of coffee, put some change down on the counter, and headed back to the station. I'd find Larry some other time.

It was all so confusing in my mind. You get ideas, you're told to look for something, and suddenly everyone looks like that something. It was no longer a matter of seeing what's out of whack but realizing unintentionally that everything was wrong and your opinions and attitudes for years weren't right. Heck, Larry's last name was Hammer which was very close to Hammerschmidt and not too far off from Suzanne Hamer. What's in a name? I could understand Evan starting to mention Larry as a possibility just because of his knowledge. But he didn't fit. There were other people who were new to town, including Ralph Houseman and Julius "Tiny" Waring, the highly unpopular science teacher at the high school. Both of them had come to town five and four years ago, respectively. It was difficult to see a maintenance man/busboy/waiter or a teacher as a saboteur, as long as you were using the movie serials as your guidelines. It was like you wanted to suspect everyone but you couldn't because then no one was a suspect. Either that or everyone was guilty.

There was a small part burning a hole deep inside, screaming for me to just leave town, vanish, disappear, head out somewhere. What if Agent Gordon had a line on me? What if an act of sabotage totally decimated the town and I could do nothing about it? There would be nothing left for me but disgrace. I was feeling more lost at that moment than any other in my life. More lost than when I came to the realization Natalie Dixon, a girl I thought I loved, brutally murdered three men in an act of horrific vengeance. This time there was nothing for me to hold onto. Sure, my fellow officers and Chief Richardson were upright men who would give their lives in defense of this city. Yet the task felt too big, more than we could handle. But I had no faith in the FBI and could only hope the military was not taking any threat lightly.

Then the true reality occurred to me—there was no place to go, nowhere I could hide. A scarred and disfigured face, a permanent mask like the mark of Cain, and I would be banished to Nod, the land east of Eden. Such a place did not exist for me nor ever would. I was bound to my destiny, a fate I had chosen many years ago. I got on that train and had to take it to the end of the line.

When I got to the station, Evan Cobb was doing his best to keep a frenzied Suzanne Hamer from completely unwinding.

"He's here. I've seen him."

"Who?"

"Eihann. My brother. I am certain I've seen him in town."

Chapter Nineteen

We brought Suzanne Hamer into the records room. There were file cabinets, a small table, and one chair filling the compact space. We practically pushed her into it, figuring she might calm down if she had nowhere to go.

"Okay, let me get this straight."

"Yes." She stumbled on the word as though it tripped up on her tongue.

"Where? Where did you see Eihann?"

"He was walking in the alley behind the hotel."

"The Osage, where you're staying?"

"Yes."

"Did you follow him?" Evan asked.

"No. I was…too scared."

"When was the last time you saw him before that, Miss Hamer?" Evan did what I would have done, asking the direct questions in hopes of getting detailed answers. He sounded fatherly, somewhat more soothing than Dave, who tended to get impatient. I tried to walk her along steadily, but we both realized she was too frantic, too upset to be a reliable witness.

"It must have been…" Her voice trailed off as though it fell into a ravine. The redness of her face faded back into a normal fleshy color, and her breathing was more regular. She paused a moment before continuing. "It was before I came to America," she replied calmly, falling apart at the recognition of reality. She had left her family for unknown reasons and did what she could to make a quiet and unassuming life for herself. The recent letters from her brother were an unwanted reminder of a discarded life, one all too clouded over with the passing years. It finally dawned on her she was a pawn in a virtually anonymous brother's wicked plan.

"Suzanne, you might have seen him. It is possible." The tone of my voice was taken directly from Dr. Brenz from nearly twenty years ago when he was doing his best to help me get through my nightmares back in the '20s, when I first came to Kansas after the war, the accident, the hospital, and all the surgeries. "But it would be difficult to be certain after such a long time. He may have changed. We all have." She looked up at me in acknowledgement. "What did he look like?" I nodded to Evan; he left to retrieve the file we had on Eihann Hammerschmidt.

"Over six foot. Sandy blond hair. He looked tan, like a man who worked outside."

"Like a farmer?"

"Yes."

"Good. What else? What kind of clothing was he wearing?"

"Something a worker would wear. Maybe even a hobo." Given he had been on the road for several days, such an appearance wouldn't surprise me. Then again, there were all kinds of workers and various kinds of clothes. It didn't give us much to go on, though I knew I couldn't press her, in the state of mind she was in. Perhaps she had seen a ghost. Whatever it may have been, it was enough to scare her.

"Was he carrying anything?"

"No. At least not that I recall."

"Did he see you?"

She looked up suddenly in what appeared to be shock or surprise.

"No."

Evan came back in the office, handed me the file, and I verified the description as given to us somewhat matched who she saw. If we had a photo, we could be more sure, but the camp did not provided us with one. We couldn't simply trust her memory. On the other hand, if she was right, Hammerschmidt was now here in town, somewhere, and things could escalate quickly, if they hadn't already.

"Evan, take Miss Hamer back to the hotel. Grab Marcus and check out the area. See if you can find Dave and have him come to Chief Richardson's office."

He nodded, and we started to step out of the file room. Looking around aimlessly was Agent Gordon standing in the middle of the hallway.

"I've got some news," he half whispered as he approached. I waved Evan on with Suzanne, who looked back apprehensively. Gordon, surprisingly, paid no attention to her. We stepped back into the file room.

"There's going to be a full inspection at Strother. Hap Arnold himself is coming." I shook my head in confusion. "Chief of the Army Air Corps. Just about the biggest bigwig there is. He's the guy who advocated the strategic bombing in Europe."

"I don't understand."

"What?"

"Burke said you two didn't think the air base would be a target, especially given their security. He said you both felt something like one of the refineries would be more accessible after I told him I was looking into Kanotex and their safety procedures."

"When did he say that?"

"I was just talking to him earlier today."

"Where?"

"Your hotel room."

Gordon moved back and forth on his feet, trying to figure out which way to go. His initial confidence upon seeing me now seemed drained. He leaned in like we were planning our own secret meeting.

"No, no, no. This is not right. Burke and I discussed Strother in depth. Looked at a set of maps of the area. Calculated there was enough there on base to warrant a review of their security measures. And this was even before I learned about General Arnold's inspection and visit. There was never, ever, any mention of an alternate target or one more viable. I don't understand."

"So where was this coming from? Was he just trying to pacify me so I would stay out of your way?"

"I don't know."

"What do you mean you don't know? You two work together."

"Yes, on this case. But he's from St. Louis. I'm from Chicago. We met up in Joplin before coming here."

There was a silence lasting about ten seconds while all the words we had spoken circled the air above us and then landed back squarely upon our heads with a thud. It was like the realization of a bomb exploding right behind you before you had a chance to react. I knew full well what that felt like. Intuitively, we both left the room and headed for the hotel. Dave Morton saw us marching out of the building and tagged along. We hopped into Agent Gordon's car and drove silently to the hotel, got out together and walked up the stairs, two at a time. We didn't need to say anything. Gordon and I were thinking the same thing.

Gordon was about to kick in the door but I grabbed his arm before he could do so.

"Key," I said. A quiet entrance would be less dangerous for those other rooms on the floor. Or maybe I just didn't want the hotel, the place where I lived as well, to have to pay for a damaged door when it wasn't necessary. The room was empty. None of Burke's things were missing, an extra suit jacket still hung in the closet, socks and underwear in the bureau drawers. We all scattered within the room, looking for something, anything that might give us an idea or indicate we were all incorrect about what seemed to be an obvious assumption. Based on our mindset of the past several days, it was doubtful anything was going to change our opinions.

It kept swirling around in my head, but I couldn't accept what I had been thinking. Burke had initially been the outgoing one, the blustering type with the big mouth, throwing his weight and that of the bureau around. If anything, I would have guessed Gordon was not on the up and up, being quiet and reserved as he was. But you never consider an FBI agent might actually be the enemy.

"I'm calling Ness." Whereas Eliot Ness no longer had the power and influence of barely ten years prior, he still had connections and would be able to help us out. He might even try to convince me again to move to

Washington and work with him. By then I might have finally become interested.

As we left the building, Cobb drove up in his car.

"We think we've found something," he said breathlessly.

"Where's Marcus?"

"He was watching a house, far end of town out east. We think we found the German."

Gordon, Dave, and I looked at each other with a slightly dampened degree of excitement by needing to determine the situation with Burke. In the back of my mind, I knew about the squatters' shacks and considered Karla Frankl might still be hanging around.

"Dave, go with them. I'll get back and call Ness, see what he can find out."

I had Linda Kuchenberg, the receptionist and switchboard operator at the station, call the direct number Eliot had given me to reach him in D.C. I could have contacted the bureau directly, but I was doubtful they would be forthcoming with any information. After all, they had two men out here in charge of a search for an escaped prisoner of war, only they didn't realize one of the men was not who he seemed to be. Maybe both. Surprisingly I got through quickly. It sounded like the cocktail hour had started early. I hoped Eliot would be lucid enough to appreciate the gravity of my current situation.

"Baron, how the heck are you?"

"We've got trouble brewing here, Eliot." I could imagine him sitting up straight and fixing his tie merely at the seriousness of my voice.

"What is it?"

"I need everything you have on a Bureau agent

named Hollis Burke. He's supposedly based out of the St. Louis office. Met up with Alexander Gordon in Joplin before coming here."

"Well, you know, you could call them directly." The dead air let Eliot know what I thought of that idea. "Yeah, you're probably right. Look, I'll ask around and see what I can find. There's a secretary or two that still thinks I'm the cat's meow."

"I'm sorry to press you on this, Eliot, but I think it has come to a head down here. This German soldier may be in town as we speak."

"I'll get right on it." He started to hang up, but I caught him.

"Oh, and Eliot?"

"Yes."

"I'll want to hear more about that job opportunity."

I couldn't see it, but I felt his smile over the phone. Hanging up, I regretted making the comment when we were in the middle of possibly opening this case wide and making an arrest. It wasn't like me to use a potential promise in exchange for something important, especially from a man I considered a friend. At this point, there was a kind of fear building up inside me I hadn't felt since the war I was in. Not even Jake Hickey made me feel that way. I could sense everything bad closing in around me: my real identity; the possibility of an act of sabotage or an assassination; perhaps even the United States losing the war because this enemy was willing to go to extreme measures with a callous disregard for any human life. The radio shows, bond tours, and big smiling faces from Hollywood might be hiding the truth about how the war could actually turn out. After all, actors were paid to act. The truth was something you could only notice in small towns like Arkansas City.

I was scared, and I was lost and knew I was capable of saying anything in such a state. That might mean saying the wrong thing. Unfortunately, I couldn't take it back now and knew I would deal with my words later. At least, that was my hope.

The four of them returned about an hour later, Marcus Hayes shaking his head.

"I don't know if I thought he went into that house or if I missed him and he snuck out of it. I was so sure we had him cornered."

"Who was it, Marcus?" I asked.

"Best as I could tell he fit the description from the Hamer woman that Cobb related. Tall, blond, workingman's clothes. Could have been a vagrant or migrant worker, for all I know."

"Or an escaped German POW," Evan retorted.

A golden opportunity wasted. But I wasn't going to let it happen.

"Take me to where you last saw him."

We drove out east of town, past the city line. We approached the area where I last saw Karla Frankl, worn down by life in general but clinging on to it nevertheless. Whereas I didn't want to get her involved, if she were even still alive, I knew there were bigger fish to fry.

Off the road to the south was a small patch of trees. I remembered a couple of shacks there, places where hunters would bed down for the night. Maybe not all that comfortable, but ideal.

The two shacks had tar-paper roofs which tended to leak, openings for windows and doors even though there were none, and dirt floors. The five of us spread out in a semicircle, trying to cover both of the buildings. The snap of a branch alerted us to one of the buildings. We moved in slowly.

Alex looked a little too eager, gun drawn and taking large steps. I grabbed his arm and held him back just as a scrawny figure ran out the back into a gun held by Dave Morton right at his face.

There was something eerily familiar about him. Skinny, almost to the point of emaciated. Glasses with lenses like Coke bottles. A smell of grease and smoke. It finally dawned on me it was Shane Burkett, the cook who worked for Tangerine Smith, the barbecue joint owner killed back in Wichita in 1938.

"Shane, what are you doing here?" I asked.

"Looking for work, boss. Ain't too much around these days."

"Well, tell you what. We'll take you over to Father David at Northside Baptist Church. He'll get you a meal and a cot. Maybe you can teach him a thing or two about cooking."

By the time we got back to town, we looked like a sorry bunch, more like rodeo clowns tossed around by wild bulls or bucking broncos. I was on the verge of the kind of headache I used to have and realized the only cures were the cheap hooch I kept in a drawer of my side table or a heaping meal at Daisy Mae's. I opted for the latter. We had to wait nearly twenty minutes to get a table that would hold five of us. Tabatha came around, smile on her face so big you couldn't tell if she just clocked in or had worked a twelve-hour shift. For the first time in a while, I felt my shoulders slack just a bit.

Things started quieting down just as our food came

out. Dixie ambled over right as I was taking a bite of an overstuffed hamburger.

"How you boys holding up? You look like you've been fighting a war."

"Just about," I responded.

"You already fought one, Baron."

"I know. Guess I can't help getting caught up in them."

She nodded in Gordon's direction. "Where's your buddy?"

"Around." Gordon, being the cagey sort, was not going to reveal all that much. Whereas we all knew Dixie and Daisy Mae's pretty well, Alex was still not willing to trust anyone, even the hash-slinging owner of the best diner in town.

"What's all the ruckus back there?" I popped my head in the direction of the kitchen.

"The base is having a to-do, day after next. They want us to bring a truck out and serve food."

"Must be Arnold's inspection," Gordon commented casually.

"They paying you well?" I asked.

"You better believe it, sonny." She slapped me on the back and walked away. I laughed and almost choked at the same time. Then I looked over at Gordon. His eyes were narrowed, head tilted toward the table, almost as though he wasn't with us.

"Gordon, what is it?"

"The diner is bringing food onto the base."

First, Marcus stopped eating, then Dave.

"Yes."

"Civilians without security clearance will be on the base."

Evan put down his chicken salad sandwich, staring in the direction of the federal agent.

"We've checked out everyone here."

"Have we? You felt the security was tight and sound. Maybe it is. But now you've got a situation where they are allowing outside individuals onto the base. Perhaps they've already got precautions in place. Or perhaps I'm being just a little too concerned."

Some thoughts were running through my head, a notion, maybe an idea. There was a slim possibility I was right but an even slimmer one I was wrong. It was up to Eliot Ness now to give me the information I needed. But it was up to all of us to locate Eihann Hammerschmidt. Even more than before, I believed Suzanne was right.

Chapter Twenty

It was time to bring Chief Richardson up to speed. I didn't want to overwhelm him with many voices spewing a bunch of unconnected facts and comments and ideas. It already sounded like a marching band in my head, and it wasn't something I wanted to share with anyone else. I couldn't help but wonder if all the ghosts from the past were trying to talk to me at once, kind of get their two cents' worth in. We sat in the chief's office, blinds drawn, with me reporting very matter-of-factly as I had done so many other times throughout the years.

"Even though the sighting didn't pan out, I have to believe Hammerschmidt is in town. Personally, I think all the blather and the letters about missing his sister down in Tulsa was a dodge."

"Agreed," he responded stoically.

"Agent Burke, on the other hand, is a mystery to me."

"So you don't think he simply has a different take on this case and is exploring other possibilities, even going so far as to withhold information from his partner?"

I shook my head, starting to doubt myself.

"I don't know either of these guys. I don't know the FBI and how they work. Ness was in the Treasury Department, so he had a whole different approach to things. These two started out coming here all hotsy-totsy, acting like we were the hoi polloi, then turn around and say no one trusts them and they need our help." I exhaled deeply. It was all terribly tiring. "Maybe they thought they could throw their weight around, but they just didn't have a clue what to expect from small town Kansas folk. I don't know, Chief. I just don't know anymore."

"You did right by calling Ness. If nothing else, you've gotten a perspective that is outside of the Bureau. And besides, they'll close ranks and probably send more agents down here. Right now, though, you need to take your team and do a secondary search in the area of this sighting. Take Gordon with you, just to keep him around. With Burke out of the picture, we need to know what at least one of these federal boys is up to. I'll make a few more calls to Camp Concordia and, well, a few fellas I know up in Topeka. And, Baron?"

"Yes, sir."

"You better have a visit with Dr. Brenz. I've noticed you've been, um, twitching again. Haven't seen that in a while."

He was probably remembering the investigation into the Wichita murders back in '38. The difficulties of the case, the pure horror of it, caused me more sleepless nights, nightmares when I could sleep, and a distinctive twitching in my face Doctie attributed to an excess of stress. I hoped to shine a light on our department by helping another jurisdiction. All it did was remind myself of all the other prior traumas in my life and made me doubt whether I was doing a darned bit of good. Back then, Dr. Brenz had given me a couple of capsules of Veronal. I had slept for nearly eighteen hours. That was how wound up I had become. It felt as though I were coming out of surgery, something all too familiar from my hospital stay in France in 1918. I didn't want to feel that way again. Ever. I just didn't want any kind of a reminder of how all of this started. There was nothing much I could do about it now. So the twitching and the dreams were my only remaining option.

Nevertheless, Chief Richardson was right. This was too important a time for me to have a physical breakdown. I went over to Doctie's office after my meeting with the chief.

He had every right to castigate me for not keeping up with my regular appointments. Of all people, Dr. Brenz was the one who helped guide me through my return from the war and get back on track with my life. He accepted me as Baron Witherspoon but was more concerned about my well-being no matter who I was or claimed to be. I often wondered if he knew the real story, the one about me starting out in life as Eric Kimble from Chicago and only taking over the identity of Baron Witherspoon, my friend from the Great War, after he died. He never let on what he knew. His duties and oaths as a physician took priority over something small and insignificant like the truth.

"There are two things which are causing the twitching. I'm not certain you can control either." He spoke to me as he had always done, with simplicity and directness. "Just as it was five years ago, you are under a great deal of stress. Now, unlike a bank manager facing an audit, you can't simply take a vacation and go camping in the Ozarks, can you?"

"We've got a war going on, Doctie. Everyone is under stress."

"Certainly." He dismissed my comment largely because I was right and there was nothing that any of us could do about it. While he could insist I take a break from my work, maybe even make it a medical requirement of my job, he knew I was not going to accept that particular prescription. "The other is simply the nature of the original surgery. Unlike Walter Yeo, who had a mask of skin transplanted across his face, your surgery involved several individual flaps of skin to cover the various lacerations and abrasions from the barbed wire. In essence, you had several masks." Dr. Brenz was recapping the surgery I knew too well, but for what purpose I didn't understand. "From all my reading, Yeo is doing well. Some minor irritation around the edges of the mask. You, Baron, have what I would call, for lack of a better explanation, a bunch of worms crawling around on your face. Or you could say under your skin. With so many flaps, it might be there is nerve damage in multiple places, thereby causing the twitching."

"Let me get this straight. Once the stress goes away, the only thing I'll have to deal with is the fact my surgery was only good for the short term and I'll wind up feeling like my flesh is melting from my face." The frustration of this investigation was unfortunately allowing me to be sarcastic about my own personal circumstances. I apologized to Dr. Brenz; he didn't deserve that.

"I understand fully what you're going through, Baron. On both fronts. As far as the stress goes, this war will not last, and you will go back to being the beloved beat cop on the Ark City police force. However, we must address the actual medical issue at some point in time. It may come to pass you will have no control over your facial muscles, might not be able to talk or eat. There could be issues with the tear ducts, causing you to—"

"Okay." I put my hand up like a traffic officer. "What do we do?" I asked calmly. I had to come to terms with the fact I was forty-five years old and had facial reconstruction surgery twenty-five years prior. I accepted my own identity, who I was both as a person and a police officer. I had no longing for any kind of warm and intimate relationship, given the failures of the past. What I could not fathom, or reason out, was what might happen to me physically. You spend most of your life figuring out who you will be and following a course of action. It is when your body fails you there is an understanding of your strengths and weaknesses. I suppose only then you find out what you're really made of.

I certainly was not the church-going type, not before in Chicago and not much here in Kansas. But I had heard of a man's "three score years and ten" from the Bible, seventy years being what was supposedly given to us. By whatever measurement you use, our time was limited. Too much of our lives are like getting lost in a wilderness. Sadly, once you emerged, you were closer to the end than the beginning.

"I've been doing some reading, Baron. When this thing is all over, we'll get together and figure out something to make sure you are more comfortable."

"I'll be looking forward to that." And I meant it. I wasn't sure where my life was going to take me when I came to Kansas, couldn't have expected to become who I had become. One thing I wanted was just a bit of normalcy and a little peace of mind. Anything else would have been a bonus.

I had no sooner stepped out of Dr. Brenz' office when Dave Morton walked up to me and said, "We got him."

Chapter Twenty-One

Dave and I got to the station about the time Marcus and Evan were leading Eihann Hammerschmidt into the building. Agent Gordon appeared almost out of nowhere, walked through the crowd of officers like Moses through the Red Sea, and guided the German forcefully by the arm to our interrogation room. He was close in appearance to Suzanne's description only he didn't look German. Then again, other than a few brute and scared kids from twenty-five years ago, my impression of Germans came from a slew of war movies Hollywood was pushing out. After all, what did they know? I stepped up my pace as well. This was our city, and I wasn't about to let the FBI take this over completely.

For the moment, it was just Gordon and me with Hammerschmidt. Initially, our prisoner looked straight ahead, barely blinking or even breathing as far as I could tell. He was definitely tough, this one, and it was going to take a great deal of pressure to get him to reveal anything, if that was even possible. I hadn't considered what kind of leverage we might have, something near and dear to him that might make him break. This kind of situation was new to me, to all of us in the department. But I had to appear as though I knew what I was doing. Otherwise, Alex Gordon was going to walk out with this guy in shackles and leave us with potentially further danger.

"You realize you're not going back to Concordia," Gordon started in a tone that almost seemed to have a Southern twang to it. "More than likely you'll be up in Leavenworth. You know what that is, right?" I could see Hammerschmidt's eyebrow rise in contempt. "They'll conduct a military trial on account of you being a soldier and all. Then they'll find you guilty of sabotage. And then, well, they'll just hang you. But I'm sure that's okay with you. After all, it was all for the Fatherland, right? *Deutschland über alles* and all that kind of Hun muck."

Hammerschmidt smiled. It was actually more like a smirk. You couldn't tell if he were being interrogated or listening to Jack Benny on the radio.

"How long have you been here?" I asked as simply as possible.

"A day. A week. A month." He was playing with us, like a cat with a ball of yarn.

"Do you find something amusing about the possibility of being executed?" I asked.

"I'd like to know exactly what I have sabotaged." He was still looking straight ahead, speaking with the calm directness of a trial lawyer.

"That's funny, because we were wondering the same thing." Gordon was playing along, only it wasn't a game.

He finally turned toward Gordon, his face grim and unrelenting, a look of condemnation shooting out like a bullet from his rifle.

"Agent Alexander Gordon. Federal Bureau of Investigation. You have captured an escaped German prisoner of war, a man desperate to reconnect with his sister who lives in Tulsa, Oklahoma." His face started to take on the look of a sad minstrel in a melodrama. "A man who has grown weary of this fighting and wishes to live in peace. I have committed no act of sabotage." For a moment, I thought there were tears in his eyes.

"How do you know who I am?"

Hammerschmidt's look of desperation faded as his smirk grew, like a funnel cloud ready to touch down on some farmer's west forty. He knew more than we did, and it gave him power.

"We know your story about your sister is a lie."

He turned toward me sharply.

"And who are you?"

I made eye contact with Gordon. Now, we had an advantage. Gordon left the room. Hammerschmidt looked at the closed door and then slowly turned his head back to me. He maintained his poise and self-control but his lack of information about me definitely had him at a disadvantage.

"She hasn't spoken to you. She knows very little of your life. And to be perfectly honest, she's rather afraid of you. Doesn't seem like an ideal situation for a reunion."

"And how do you know all this, Officer—?"

"Witherspoon." I recited my name as though it were one of the archangels.

"How do you know so much about my sister, Officer Witherspoon?"

"Because I have spoken with her in depth." There was a look of doubt on his face, that I was some sort of yokel who was ribbing him. "Your whole story is a farce. You escaped for the sole purpose of coming here to commit an act of sabotage. Now, to my knowledge, that makes you a spy. Especially when you consider you were wearing neither a military uniform nor a prisoner's garb. And just like your country, we execute spies. So you see, you won't get the chance to do what you planned."

"And how do you know I'm not the only one who escaped?"

I shook my head dismissively, like I was scolding a child or a puppy.

"You really want me to answer the question?" I sat in the other chair in the room, just to the side of the table he was sitting at. I was no longer above him. We were on an eye-to-eye level. However, from where I sat, he was forced to turn his head toward me, giving up a certain sense of superiority if only temporarily. "Look, whatever is going to happen, if it happens at all, is going to happen without you. You'll wait out the rest of the war in a cold prison cell, ultimately realizing you let a good situation slip from your fingers."

"A bird in a gilded cage?" He was trying to sound defiant, attempting to regain an emotional strength to exert his supposed superiority.

"Call it what you will. But from what I've seen, not everyone from this so-called master race is a master of his own fate."

He cleared his throat, sat upright, and tugged on his shirt, straightening it and himself out.

"I am Oberfeldwebel Eihann Hammerschmidt of the German army. My duty is to my country. It is my responsibility to uphold and carry out the orders given to me by the High Command. I will not shirk from that responsibility."

"Buddy, your responsibility is in the privy along

with all the other crap."

He looked straight ahead. As far as he was concerned, we had concluded our discussion. Short of a sap, he wasn't going to reveal anything, and it was doubtful that would have done much good anyway. Part of me couldn't help but smile on the inside. The good soldier in the face of abject failure was maintaining his loyalty and his pride. Nothing good was going to come of it.

I took a peek behind the blinds and caught Marcus Hayes' attention. He came in, and I went out. Agent Gordon paced angrily. He might have had a notion to rough up the German if we weren't around. At least, that's the way I imagined it. I wonder how well it would have sat with Hoover.

"You didn't get anything, did you?" he spat.

"No."

"What do you plan to do?"

I stared at Gordon, not actually at him but in his direction. I was lost in thought for a moment, trying to get something in the back of my head to pop forward.

"Cobb, where did you find this guy?"

"There's the old Welch place on Elm between 6th and 7th."

"Yeah, I know it. Got repossessed by the bank back before the war. It has gone to heck in a hand basket. I don't even think the bank has tried to sell it. They certainly haven't tried to fix it up, either."

"We heard someone rummaging around, took a look inside, and grabbed him."

"You have any idea what he was looking for?"

"Food, probably."

There was something sticking in my head I

couldn't place. Why was Hammerschmidt there? The area was a good spell away from the Kanotex Refinery or any of the packing plants and certainly a good spell away from the main air base or the auxiliary field. It just wasn't an area we figured would be a target. I suppose an abandoned house might have had some food, but it was doubtful. My best guess was they used the house as either a place to sleep or a meeting spot.

Linda Kuchenberg ran for the first time since I'd known her. She only traversed about forty feet but she was out of breath, shaking a notepad at me to get my attention as though her belabored breathing wasn't enough.

"Baron, it's Mr. Ness."

I looked over at Gordon.

"Patch it through to the chief's office."

We went together, me advising Chief Richardson there might be some news. He handed me the phone.

"Baron, you got a mess on your hands."

"Tell me about it." I thought I had previously made that clear to Eliot, who had a tendency toward grandiose statements of the obvious.

"No, I mean for real." The seriousness of his voice was like a splash of ice-cold water.

"How so?"

"The FBI is all over Joplin. They found the body of Agent Hollis Burke south of town in an area called Wildcat Glades. He'd been shot in the back of the head twice."

"An execution." The words fell out of my mouth like marbles. It was something I was aware of from so very long ago.

"Whoever you've got there is certainly no FBI

agent."

I thanked Eliot and hung up. I must have had a look of terror on my face when I looked at Gordon and spouted, "We might have Operation Pastorius all over again" before filling him and the chief in on the details.

We went back to the interrogation room.

"Lock him up someplace dark," I barked at Marcus, "and then join us out front."

Hammerschmidt looked at me with a confused defeat on his face, eyes blank and not as intimidating as before. He had been our focus until just a few moments before, and now he was like trash brought to the city dump. His lack of importance seemed to fill him with dread. He was in the privy along with his soldier's responsibility.

There was Dave, Evan, and Marcus, along with Agent Gordon and me, left after the German was put in a holding cell with a beat cop to guard him.

"The guy that calls himself Agent Burke, he's our guy."

"Who is he?" Dave asked. We all turned toward Gordon.

"Don't know," he responded.

"Why not?"

"Like I said before, we met up in Joplin after receiving our individual orders."

"From who?"

"The SAC in Joplin."

Evan had his face scrunched up almost worse than mine. "What's a SAC?"

"Special Agent in Charge," Gordon spat, almost annoyed at this moderate interrogation.

"What's his name?" I continued, trying desperately

to figure out exactly what was going on.

"Art Grantham."

"You ever met him before?"

"No."

"This Burke, did he act like anything other than an FBI agent?" I asked.

"No. We talked about the investigation. He made comments. I made comments. That was it. Nothing out of the ordinary I hadn't done with any other agent I've ever worked with. It's not like we check each other's credentials."

"So you have no idea who this guy really is?"

"If you say he's not Burke, I haven't got a clue."

Gordon and I headed back to the hotel and reviewed every paper and report they had accumulated. I gave instructions that Marcus, Evan, and Dave were each to partner up with another beat officer and reconnoiter what we considered the possible targets we had previously figured.

"What about Strother Field?" Dave asked before we left.

"For now, let's assume they've got their security taken care of. We need to focus on places that don't have armed guards protecting them."

"What about the bigwig that's supposed to be coming there?"

"There are too many other targets out there." I looked at the clock on the wall. "We meet back here at five o'clock."

It felt like time was moving a whole lot faster than it had been.

Chapter Twenty-Two

Five o'clock came around like an arrow from a restless Indian's bow. It was usually quitting time for most shifts. No one was quitting now or had any intention of the sort.

We gathered in the biggest room we had, every cop that had been out scouring the city for something, anything. Chief Richardson had been busy making phone calls to just about anyone who would listen. The governor's office had not been informed of the FBI's presence in Arkansas City nor did they get any reports from Camp Concordia or any of the other prisoner-of-war camps in the state. The Kansas Highway Patrol had not encountered anything that could remotely resemble any acts of sabotage in any of the smaller communities around the state. The chief had gotten through to some administrator in Henry Stimson's office, the Secretary of War. Everyone's feedback amounted to a whole lot of nothing, doubletalk, and the general stuff politicians say. All I got was smooth indifference after a quick call to Detective Rackler up in Wichita. We were as lost as we could be.

The only things we had sounded like the makings of a vaudeville routine. There was a captured German POW with a background in munitions and who claimed to be seeking a reunion with his sister, which we didn't buy in the least. The other character was a phony FBI agent whose identity was unknown but who assuredly was involved in whatever plan we knew nothing about and were trying to stop. Finally, a variety of potential targets including an Army air base we had to assume was secured, given the fact they had more personnel and arms than our entire police department. This was no radio serial. We weren't able to tune in next week to find out what happened in the cliffhanger. Whatever we thought, we were certain some act of sabotage was going to take place sooner rather than later.

"May I suggest something?" Gordon's tone was soft and tranquil, almost like a dying man at peace with his forthcoming passing.

"Go ahead."

"However disorganized we might be, realize these people are not. This fake Burke was a meticulous plant. As you alluded, I can't even be sure Art Grantham is the SAC in Joplin and if my orders were valid. This German POW had a definitive plan, perhaps several alternative sites. He did not head toward Canada or Mexico. I agree with your assessment there is a probable co-conspirator, perhaps more than one, somewhere in the community. The phony Burke would not be able to carry out anything on his own since he is not from the area. I surmise he was here to ensure Hammerschmidt and the other plant would be able to unite and continue their mission."

"What if it was nothing more than a suicide mission?" Marcus interjected. "You know, load up a car with explosives, crash the gate of the target, and drive it into a building. Kapow!"

"Possible," Gordon responded, "but unlikely. The German *Abwehr* is about intelligence gathering and sabotage, not suicide missions. No, we will need to ferret out the likeliest co-conspirators more than finding this fake Burke."

"You haven't mentioned the most likely co-conspirator," I said slyly.

Gordon looked at me, first blank-faced, before an equally sly smile appeared.

"I was wondering when you were going to get around to making such a comment."

"What would you do in my position?"

"Don't let me out of your sight." The sly smile remained. If he wasn't a German agent, I felt pretty sure Alex Gordon might just become head of the FBI some day. I turned my attention to the small team of men who had worked diligently throughout this.

"Evan, whittle down the list we made to, let's say, the five best options. We'll bring them in as, I don't know…material witnesses."

"To what?"

"Make something up. We need them in here." I turned toward Agent Gordon. "What do you suppose the fake Burke is doing now?"

"He's waiting."

"Waiting for what?"

"He knows what's going on, probably knows we caught Hammerschmidt. He's in position right now. He could be waiting for the tools to carry out the mission, maybe turn it over to the other conspirator, or simply looking for an ideal vehicle for an escape. One thing is for sure. He's not on the run like a rabid dog. These men have a military-style plan to carry out. They have deception on their side."

"But we know about the fake Burke."

"Yes, but we don't know who his partner or partners are. And there are still many people who don't know Burke is a fake. With those credentials, he might be able to gain access to something necessary to his cause before we can get around to stopping him or warning others."

I was feeling like sand in an hourglass running down into the lower half. I turned to Chief Richardson for support, advice, a comment. Something. Anything.

"I know how important all of this is," he said, picking up where I left off, "but I can see you're all pretty ragged. You won't be able to think much or respond appropriately if you don't get a night's rest and something to eat." He sounded more like a mother than the chief of police, but he had a point. We worked out a rotational set of four-hour shifts between Dave, Marcus, and Evan and their beat officer partners, bringing in potential co-conspirators and talking with them, then making a sweep of the city just to keep our presence felt. Alex and I took the first shift.

We were headed over to Tony Creamer's place when Suzanne came up to us.

"I've got to talk to you." There seemed to be tears forming in her eyes, and she appeared a bit desperate. We were too far to head back to the station, so I simply pulled her aside.

"What is it?"

"I'm scared."

"Of what?"

"Of Eihann."

I smiled at her, trying my best to be reassuring. "He's in custody, held in a cell, and on twenty-four-hour watch. It was one thing to walk off a work detail.

But he's not getting out of our jail. I guarantee it."

"He was here to do something bad. He used me, used my name and the fact I was his sister, to convince people to trust him."

"Suzanne, he is a German soldier. He trained for this. But no one here trusts him."

Suddenly, she hugged me, not anything romantic, more like a desperate grab, as though she were holding on to a life raft in a thrashing storm. She was cold, like a corpse, but her heart beat like a clock whose springs had burst. I felt more like an older brother at that point, the true and honorable brother who would not betray her. She, too, had run from her past and was content to live a quiet, unimaginative life, if only to have a little peace of mind. It was something I understood and could embrace completely. I let her hold me for as long as she needed.

"Head on back to the hotel. I'll have officers check up on you periodically."

"I'm not opening the door for anyone but you."

She turned defiantly and marched off. I couldn't tell any longer if she was in jeopardy or in control. I realized I was smiling for the first time in a while.

"That's something you don't need right now," Gordon said quietly.

I nodded in agreement. We continued on to find Tony Creamer.

"If Burke was a phony," I said out of the blue, picking up on my earlier comments, "how do I know you're not as well?" This time, as we were alone, I felt the need to be more direct.

He smiled wickedly.

"You don't. How do I know you're who you say

you are?"

Alexander Gordon had not impressed me as a man who liked playing games. He came here initially quite reserved and withdrawn, contemptuous for a reason I still couldn't define. However, he had opened up once or twice, showed his human side. It occurred to me spies tried more to hide in the shadows than walk in the light. I needed to be able to trust him and was hoping he would give me a reason.

"If you bust this case, what will it do for your career in the FBI?"

"Not much. There are many I work with who think Jews should be lawyers or bankers and are not equipped to be field agents who can fire guns and kill people. I'd venture to say there are many I work with who don't trust me because I am a Jew."

"But you'll prove them wrong."

"You can write it in stone," he proclaimed stoically, looking straight ahead, perhaps at his future.

Alex let me do the talking with Tony Creamer. I started out by letting him know we were aware his real name was Anton Kreutzer and he was originally from Austria. He immediately panicked, but I calmed him down by telling him we needed his help. Did he know any other Austrians or Germans who had come over around the same time? What was the attitude of the other Austrians or Germans he knew? Did any of them share the beliefs of the Nazis? The questions then went into what he did at the packing plant, what materials he had access to, where he had been for the last twenty-four hours. He didn't appear to feel he were some kind of suspect even though our questions were in that vein. Alex looked at him, watching his face as he responded.

We left after a half hour. Outside, Alex lit a cigarette and shook his head.

"It's not him. He's a laborer with no definable skills. And he voted for Roosevelt three times."

"What now?"

"You tell me, Officer Witherspoon."

We continued up and down side streets, keeping our eyes and ears open. Walking down Elm, we passed the location where we had picked up Hammerschmidt. I still couldn't pinpoint why it seemed familiar. It felt like a mosquito buzzing in my ear.

Chapter Twenty-Three

It was a morning similar to one five years prior. Back then, I woke up in the Eaton Hotel, refreshed after a stressful day and yet confused at my surroundings, actually oblivious to where I was. That, however, was different. It was somewhere unfamiliar. This morning I awoke in the place I had called home for several years. Somehow, for the first time, it felt strange.

Perhaps it was the notion of the man we thought was Agent Hollis Burke was not him at all. I encountered so many instances of this, the deception that man was capable of, like Jake Hickey and Ronnie Roché. Well, I suppose when I considered Natalie Dixon, it was women as well. And, of course, I was no less guilty. I had become Baron Witherspoon through time and through my actions. What would residents of Arkansas City say if they knew the truth? What would Dave Morton and Chief Richardson say? In the end, would it truly make a difference?

But this fake Agent Burke was another matter altogether. He was likely a collaborator somehow with the German army, perhaps German himself. At the very least, he was an unscrupulous man who killed an FBI agent for the purposes of carrying out a plot against the citizens of a small Kansas town who were guilty of nothing more than being patriotic citizens. Just Americans who happened to be the enemy in this gigantic global war. If captured, he would certainly be tried and executed. Maybe that mattered to him; maybe it didn't. I was certain of one thing: he would stay the course and carry out his desperate act. For that reason alone, we had to stop him.

I met Agent Gordon in the lobby and we agreed to head on over to Daisy Mae's for some breakfast. After the chief's order of a good night's sleep, he would probably want us to have full bellies as well, and there was not a better place in town to get that done.

It was not as crowded as it had typically been ever since Strother Field opened. On any given morning, there were American, French, and Brazilian pilots gobbling up some of the best breakfast anyone was going to find in a fifty-mile radius. This morning it was largely the locals. I called Dixie over to find out what was going on.

"Remember they got that big to-do at the air field? Some bigwig yahoo coming in. I sent Ralph over this morning with the truck and a bunch of food. They figure it's safer for the big shot to eat his hamburgers from town on the base than waddle around among us little people."

"And, as far as I'm concerned, the food here is probably a darn sight better than any of the slop they serve on the base."

As soon as the words were out of my mouth, my face went numb. Not as though it were something to do with the scarring, more like the blood draining from me and leaving me cold. Like a dream, I pictured in my head the Welch house where we picked up Hammerschmidt. It was as though I was looking at a map. Some point was sticking in my head like an ice pick. I remembered giving Ralph Houseman a ride home one night when he got out late from work. He lived in a rooming house on 6th and Oak, just one block north. He was someone who showed up out of nowhere five years ago, without much of a background to speak of or that anyone had even asked about, about the time when Hitler just started to extend his grasp in Europe but before the United States was actively involved. He was someone who was often described as "good with his hands," "a good worker," and "a guy who knows how to get things done." And right now, he was on the Strother Army Air Field base with a truck that was supposed to contain food.

"It's Houseman." My words were sharp, clear, and direct. We left our plates of biscuits and gravy behind, leaving as quickly as a Kansas twister when it was done doing its damage.

We drove back to the municipal building and found Dave and his sidekick coming back from a sweep of the north side of town. I explained to him what I remembered. I yelled to Linda Kuchenberg to call Marcus and Evan, who were sleeping after their shifts. We told her to have them pick up rifles and shotguns here at the station and meet us at Strother. We went to the basement where the armory was. I grabbed a shotgun and Dave a Tommy gun. Alex loaded his revolver, making sure he had extra bullets in his pocket. I drove with Alex while Dave came in a police car.

We pulled up in front of the gates. Several MPs were on guard, more so than when we had visited previously. This was largely due to General Hap Arnold's appearance and inspection. Alex figured his status would gain us entrance.

"I'm Special Agent Gordon with the FBI," he declared, showing his credentials. "We believe an armed man has accessed the base with the intention of sabotage or potentially the assassination of General Arnold."

"Impossible, sir," one MP with blond curly hair and a big-toothed grin replied. "The base is secure as Fort Knox." If he hadn't been an MP, he would have been in college, part of a fraternity, pulling pranks like panty raids or stuffing phone booths. Instead, he was all that was standing between us and a possible tragedy.

"Did a food truck from a local diner come in this morning?" I pleaded.

"I just got on an hour ago. But I can check."

"Yes. Do so." My reply was less a request than an order. This squeaky-clean kid had no idea what was going on. He ambled into the guard shack on the other side of the gate.

In the time it took the MP to make a phone call to someone who could really authorize our access, Marcus, Evan, and two other officers showed up. We waited as patiently as we could, knowing something bad could happen at any moment and fearing we could do nothing about it.

The MP ambled back to the gate, which remained locked, barring us from entering.

"Well, yeah, there is a truck from a place called Daisy Mae's here. Supposed to be serving up food at lunch."

"Yes, that's it." I was practically yelling now.

"He's been cleared. The truck checked out. I think you fellas are mistaken."

"Get Major Vance on the phone. Now." Gordon's

voice was gruff and hoarse. The MP just didn't understand. His pace quickened a bit at the sudden outburst, only now realizing we were talking about an urgent matter. He brought the bag phone over and handed it through the wires to Gordon.

"Major Vance, there will be an act of sabotage committed sometime within the next hour if we are not allowed to come onto the base and address it." Gordon nodded and said "uh-huh" a couple of times before handing the phone back to the MP, whose face got red pretty quick. They opened the gate, and a jeep with four more MPs pulled up. Alex and I greeted them quickly.

"Major Vance wants this handled with discretion." The MP who spoke seemed more like a Harvard graduate than a seasoned soldier. He treated this as though it were a Hollywood premiere. "Under no circumstances are you to interrupt the inspection by General Arnold…"

"Just help us find the truck." Gordon interrupted.

One MP went with each group of two of us. They gave us directions as to where on the base the truck might have been after it was determined it moved from its originally sanctioned location. We were to take a circuitous route around the outer edge of the base with a plan to head toward the middle where the inspection was taking place. The thought was any assassination attempt would be from the vantage point of a trained sniper, something none of the police officers were aware of or could even guess about. Gordon looked in every direction. It dawned on me he might have the best idea where this would be.

It was so much different than weaving through the forests in France. At least there were places to hide. For the most part, other than buildings and barracks and hangars, the base was wide open. That would make it tough for a sniper. It would also leave us without any cover should we wind up turning into targets.

We found the truck parked at the side of a maintenance building. It was well within sight of the main grounds, where many of the pilots lined up in neat rows as General Arnold walked up and down. The first thing I noticed was Dave, the other police officer with him, and an MP coming up from the front end of the truck. The second thing I noticed was something sticking out of the back of the truck. It was a rifle.

There was no time to figure out what to do. I ran toward the truck, weaving back and forth. Dave had done the same thing from the front. He was at the back right of the truck and could see the door slightly ajar. I was on the left side. If either of us tried to move to the back of the truck, we could have drawn fire and been shot while the other would be able to take out Ralph. I wasn't in a sacrificial mood that day. I didn't expect Dave to be either.

"Ralph," I shouted. "You're surrounded. Come out with your hands up."

It was just a thing to say. I knew he wouldn't follow instructions. Whoever he was, his mission was more important than his life, and we both knew it.

The rifle shot came through the panel of the truck and missed my head by two inches. It was the only distraction Dave needed to jump around to the back and fire at him with the Tommy gun. I pumped off two blasts from the shotgun for safe measure.

A bunch of airmen and MPs ran toward us after the sound of the gunfire. Dave and I slowly looked into the truck to find Ralph Houseman, or whoever he really was, cut to ribbons by the bullets. Alex came, and met up with Major Vance, who recommended a sweep of the base for any ordnance that could cause an explosion. After all, there were gasoline reserves of over two hundred thousand gallons just hanging around.

The saboteur was dead but somehow it didn't feel as though everything was over and we could close the chapter. Alex and I looked at each other thinking the same thing: Where was the fake Burke?

Chapter Twenty-Four

It was just the two of us, Agent Gordon and me, walking toward the front gate. As we spoke, our pace quickened.

"He wouldn't have been able to get in," I commented.

"He had FBI credentials and we never made the base aware he was a fake."

"He wouldn't have known that. No, he would have assumed he had been identified."

"You can't assume anything with these types, Baron."

"So?"

Agent Gordon's head moved around like an owl, scoping out the landscape and trying to make a determination of what could be transpiring.

"Getaway car," he declared. I thought he was talking about gangsters like Jake Hickey. "Like I've said, these are not necessarily suicide missions."

"Looked awful like a suicide mission with Ralph."

"He didn't expect to get made so quickly. With these guys, it's very well planned and very detailed. Their intention is to complete their mission and escape. Maybe do more damage elsewhere."

"So he's either on base, if he was able to convince them he was an FBI agent, or he's waiting outside."

"Assuming he hasn't already driven off after the

sound of the gunfire."

"Maybe he didn't hear it." I was hoping against hope.

I turned at the sound of approaching footsteps. It was Dave Morton.

"That Burke fella may be on base," I said.

"How?" Dave responded.

"He had his badge as an FBI agent." Dave nodded in understanding. "Continue your sweep inside the base. Make a hundred percent sure it's clear."

"What am I looking for?"

"A fast car."

Alex and I were going to reconnoiter outside. Our best chance was the fake Burke was sequestered somewhere far enough away to have not heard the commotion deep inside the base. If we were wrong, he was likely long gone.

The road into the base came off State Highway 77, but there were also side roads from the entryway before you got to the front gate. Chances are he would have been there, either slightly to the north or to the south, parallel with the state highway. This would have placed him close enough to gain access to a main road but far enough away from the base where he would not have been so obvious.

Alex had parked his car just fifteen feet in front of the main gate of the base. He would head to the south and I to the north. After a bit, we decided if we didn't find him, we would get in his car and park ourselves out near 77, knowing he would have to come by us at some point.

There was quite a bit of brush up in my area, not enough to hide a car completely and yet too much to make it easy to drive off in a hurry. After the multiple gunshots and the clambering of feet, the air was still and quiet. It reminded me of battles in France, right before they began. The loneliness could be felt as nothing moved, a tranquility based on fear and uncertainty, a silence that was made to be broken, and without warning. It was the sound of death.

Two gunshots. A black sedan speeding first north, then east toward the state highway, followed by Alex Gordon yelling, "It's him."

We jumped into his car and followed in a high-speed pursuit. We were able to catch up and get within sight of the fake Burke within a minute or two. He made a sharp turn to the right onto 202nd Road and then turned north, onto a county road I recalled from so many years ago. The one where I drove Will Bell up to Winfield. The same road George McAlister drove "Crazy" Jake Hickey on when he, Hickey, double-crossed and killed him. This road was nothing but trouble and bad memories. It was likely more would be made today.

It was also a road that didn't take too well to fast cars. County roads were rough dirt, no gravel, and no pavement. Most weren't even graded for anything more than a tractor. Many a car had a tire blown or an axle broken just driving normal on it. The black sedan was going close to fifty miles an hour.

A sharp bend in the road at such a speed caused the car to veer off into a ditch. Because it didn't flip over, the fake Burke got out after the car wouldn't start and ran toward a wheat field. His black clothing made him stick out like a sore thumb. It was apparent he didn't belong here.

Gordon calmly stopped the car, got out, and reached into the back seat. He pulled out what I recognized was a .30 Springfield Sporter. It was something I remembered from boot camp and the forests of France. Only a trained sniper would be using something so powerful. I figured that was the case, the way he had been looking around inside the base. At that moment, I had a new appreciation for Special Agent Alex Gordon.

The man we knew as Hollis Burke kept running, did not turn back to fire his revolver, and really did not seem to want to do anything but run. Alex got down on one knee, lined up his rifle, took a deep breath before taking aim. It only took one shot to bring him down. My eyes lit up with both admiration and fear.

We both went at a good pace to see where he had fallen. It took a bit to catch up to him, due to his head start. With his rifle slung over his shoulder, Alex jogged up to where the man lay face down. The shot had entered high between his shoulder blades. Even with the black jacket, we saw the deeper red saturating his back like thick sweat. He pushed with both arms, trying desperately to turn over. Gordon rolled the rifle off his shoulder and lined it up in case he still had a weapon in his hand. I aimed my gun at the man's head. I had learned to expect anything from these types.

Finally he pushed himself over. It was then we saw the bullet had come out through his throat. There was a raspy muttering mixed with a gurgling sound, followed by wheezing and strained breathing.

"Who are you?" Alex barked. "Who are you?" They could hear that shout all the way in Washington D.C.

The man was able to force a smirk on his face, the kind of sinister smile those with secrets are willing to bring with them to their death. I had known several people who passed away leaving more questions than answers. That was regrettably what happened. A last breath left his body and floated away to a distant hiding place while blood spurted out of his mouth and nearly covered the clownish smile.

"Well, Purvis got his and I got mine."

Gordon spit in the direction of the body. His disgust was evident, given the fact both this imposter and Ralph Houseman died in an effort to commit war crimes on United States soil, and he could do nothing more than etch another notch in the ledger. I'm sure he was upset at the notion he was fooled by this hulking man into the belief they were both working for the same cause. No man likes to be taken. This was true of Alex Gordon.

He walked back slowly to the car. He had the rifle slung back over his shoulder. There was a lightness in his step, as though we had been out hunting rabbits and would now have something to cook for dinner. Gordon placed the rifle gingerly in the back seat, as though he were putting a baby to bed. He wiped his brow with a handkerchief and let out a heavy sigh.

"I was there with Purvis in Ohio in '34," he started, as though reciting the words to an old poem. A slight laugh escaped his lips as he spoke. "One month on the job, a fresh-faced graduate of Queens College. You know, my dad wanted me to be a lawyer and stay close to home." He nodded at the memory. "I didn't see too much of a future in the legal field. I figured I could make my mark in law enforcement. Same but different, maybe. Dad didn't much like it when I joined the Bureau." He smiled fully, relishing his youthful rebellion like a rite of passage. "I got a call early in the morning and was told to join Purvis in Cincinnati to help with the kidnapping of a Kentucky woman. Well, just about as I got there, they notified Purvis that Floyd was in Ohio. Right then and there, without so much as a how-do-you-do, we all got on a chartered plane and headed out."

He turned away from me, looking back toward the field where the dead imposter lay. Maybe he was trying to look back on a field somewhere in his past only it was too far to see.

"I had the highest rating for marksmanship, even more than some of the guys who had been snipers in the war. I'll bet you didn't know that. I really felt like Purvis trusted me. Nevertheless, when Floyd was running in open field and I raised my rifle, he turned back toward me like an angry father. I stood down and he took the shot. I learned then it was not about doing what was right. It was all about the headlines. That is the way Hoover wanted it back then. Who knows? Probably now as well." He turned back and glared at me as though I were Purvis or maybe his own father. "So now I get credit for taking down someone who has no identity. Not much to hang my hat on, wouldn't you say, Officer Witherspoon?"

At that moment, I was feeling kind of paternal. All the years that passed gave me a sensation of having gone through a baptism of fire. All the times I felt lost, I found myself once again. I knew what Agent Alex Gordon was experiencing. I hoped he would come out clean on the other side.

"We stopped conspirators of the Germans from killing soldiers, officers, civilians, and maybe even prevented a catastrophe that would have taken innocent lives. No, it wouldn't have impacted the war effort if they had succeeded. But we saved lives. We're going to win this one, Alex. I'm not in this for the headlines. Are you?"

He looked at me and nodded. At the end of the day, our side won and we were both still alive. That's all we needed to hang our hat on.

Chapter Twenty-Five

In the next couple of days, a contingent from Camp Concordia, including a Sergeant Price and a Private Friebus, as well as three army MPs, came to the station early. Manacles attached to hands and legs replaced the handcuffs from the Arkansas City police. They were going to ensure this particular prisoner of war would not escape again. Everything was businesslike, and the business was military.

"Where are you taking him?" I asked casually.

"A more secure facility, sir," responded Sergeant Price. He did not have the slightest emotion on his face or seem to care for any. I figured the answer was satisfactory. Oberfeldwebel Eihann Hammerschmidt would no longer be trusted to remain at Camp Concordia among the other soldiers who were truly content to wait out the war. Birds in gilded cages, perhaps, but still alive and with some dignity. While there was no actual proof of his attempt to commit sabotage, Hammerschmidt's status as an escaped prisoner of war would effectively keep him out of the action for the remainder of the conflict, his fate to be determined by agencies far above our meager police departments. This was the mission he accepted and the price he would pay.

He turned his head as they started to take him away, looking at me with a contempt I had not seen from anyone before. This in spite of his lack of success.

"It goes on," he said.

"What does?"

"The war."

I walked up to him, showing a contempt I'd never had before.

"Perhaps. But it will end. And you will be left to wonder what to do with whatever remains of your life. You see, men like you live for hatred and anger. You have no use in a peacetime world. After the war, you will fade like all the rest."

"You are wrong, Officer Witherspoon. Hatred and anger will survive long after this war has ended. Even in your so-called peacetime. And I will still be around to relish it."

I nodded to the army men to take him away. I was fearful of what I could do or say next. The disgust at feeling my own hate and anger was gagging my throat. When I turned around, Alex Gordon stood behind me, practically laughing.

"You feel better?" he asked mockingly.

"No."

"You know, you're not going to win with those types. Even shackled and being taken off to a secure prison, he still thinks he's won."

"Hasn't he?"

"How? He's going to sit out the rest of the war in a cold stone cell wondering how he could have made a difference. That will eat him up alive. But I'll tell you who did win."

"Oh?"

"Guys like Ralph and the fake Hollis Burke. They're the ones you have to be scared of. You see, you can't tell who they are, and you can't tell what side they're on. They stand in front of you like a long-time buddy until you turn around. Then they stab you in the back. Or worse. They're the real danger, Baron."

I walked with him out of the station and to his car parked out front.

"Heading back to Chicago?" I asked.

"No. Washington. The director wants me to head up an investigation of enemy infiltration into the ranks. I guess I'm going to be a spy hunter."

"Not bad for a Jew, huh?"

"It's just another step. Not all the way, but I'll take it for now. I'm going to have Hoover's job one of these days." The smile was slightly whimsical. Maybe he believed what he said or maybe it was just for personal motivation. He started to get into his car, then looked over the top at me. He had a look on his face as if he wanted to say something but was really trying to hold back from doing so. "When I started in the Bureau, a couple of the old-timers told me about the heyday in Chicago. You know, when Capone was running things. They said that most of the North Side Gang, guys like Dion O'Banion and Hymie Weiss, started out as pickpockets and sneak thieves."

"Is that a fact?" His knowledge—but more where he was going—intrigued me.

"A lot of them became gangsters and caused a whole bunch of trouble for a number of years. When the heat was on, they hid out in Arkansas and Missouri and, well, Kansas. Some of them even took it upon themselves to muscle in on towns like Ark City. You know, like Jake Hickey tried to do. Figured if they couldn't be butter-and-egg men in Shy Town they'd find their fortune in the sticks." He sounded sappy trying to talk in a lingo out of his league and many years gone.

"Oh, I'm sure a lot of them found the straight path as well."

"You think so?" he asked.

"I know so."

He smiled before he got in his car and drove off. I was pretty certain he had no interest in coming back. His future lay elsewhere, a place he could make his mark and stand out.

Last time I checked the papers, the war was still going on. While the Allies had taken Guadalcanal and Tunisia and the Russians had taken back Stalingrad, battles were still intense and bloody. We would have to pummel the enemy into submission. Based on my own experience, there were still infiltrators to be wary of, and they came in all shapes and sizes.

The only thing that would take my mind off this was a hearty breakfast at Daisy Mae's. Dixie was behind the counter, as two girls had called in sick. Fortunately for her, the short order cook was healthy; otherwise I would only have been able to get toast and bacon.

I sat in a booth opposite Larry Hammer, who calmly drank his coffee. He didn't seem rattled by anything past, present, or future.

"You know, the escaped soldier we caught, his name was Hammerschmidt. Any relation to you?" I thought I'd try to see if I could throw him off just once.

"My family is English."

"Well, what do you know?" Larry knew that I knew. We both smiled. I never had any doubt about

Larry Hammer and I never would.

Dixie brought over a plate of biscuits and gravy, fried eggs, and sausage links. I was going to revel in this breakfast. To my surprise, she sat down alongside Larry.

"You glad that's all over, Baron?"

"It ain't."

"What do you mean?"

"Ever since I've been a cop, there's always been something. Farmers State Bank Robbery in '25. Jake Hickey in '34. Those murders in '35. Yeah, this war will end, but there'll still be a lot of work to do."

Arkansas City was not a crime-ridden burg, not wholly run by bootleggers and corrupt politicians like Joplin or Kansas City or Hot Springs. We'd had our share, of course, but for the most part it was a good town to live in and, if you were of a mind for it, to raise a family.

In the nearly twenty-five years I had been here, I came to be who I am. For the longest time I was lost, just trying to hide from something or someone I thought might be chasing me. In the end, it was only a memory I had been looking at in my rearview mirror.

"Bugs" Moran was in jail after trying to make and cash American Express checks. Capone had completed his jail term and was living in his estate in Florida, a man broken in spirit and body. "Machine Gun Kelley" was in Alcatraz. So was "Creepy" Karpis. The rest of the North Side Gang was dead.

I had found a place in this world far from the past. For better or worse.

A word from the author...

I studied film-making and creative writing at the University of Miami in the '80s, was involved in the Boston Poetry Scene in the '90s, and am a former president of the Kansas Writers' Association. My work has stretched from crime fiction to poetry, screen writing to experimental fiction.

I live in a 100+-year-old Victorian home in Wichita, KS with my wife, Shelia, and Sir Pounce Alot (the orange manx) and Lady Mittens (the tuxedo manx).

Find me at:

http://tikiman1962.wordpress.com

https://hbberlow.com/